"What are [you doing?" she] **asked, a flash of anger that he made her feel this way burning in her chest.**

"To take you," Sebastian said, so softly. *Too softly.*

Her skin reacted to the caress of his voice and the word *take* before her brain could change the definition.

Heated images of what it meant to be taken by him, what it had felt like to be his, stole her breath. But she would not soften under his gaze. She wouldn't let herself remember how good it had felt. She'd only let herself remember the hurt of his rejection.

It *still* hurt.

She stiffened her spine. "I'll never be *taken* by you again."

"Oh, but you will be," he said. He moved closer until her neck ached from looking up so high.

"I will take you," he said again.

Her mouth parted on a silent exhale. Despite her tough words, her body remembered for her.

She leaned, *only slightly*, but enough to feel the pressure increase. And she tingled beneath his hand as he told her exactly what else he meant to take.

"And *my* baby."

Lela May Wight grew up with seven brothers and sisters. Yes, it was noisy, and she often found escape in romance books. She still does, but now she gets to write them, too! She hopes to offer readers the same escapism when the world is a little too loud. Lela May lives in the UK with her two sons and her very own hero, who never complains about her book addiction—he buys her more books! Check out what she's up to at lelamaywight.com.

Books by Lela May Wight

Harlequin Presents

His Desert Bride by Demand
Bound by a Sicilian Secret
The King She Shouldn't Crave
Italian Wife Wanted

Visit the Author Profile page at Harlequin.com.

KIDNAPPED FOR HER SECRET

LELA MAY WIGHT

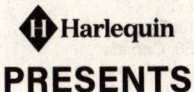

PRESENTS

If you purchased this book without a cover you should be aware that this book is stolen property. It was reported as "unsold and destroyed" to the publisher, and neither the author nor the publisher has received any payment for this "stripped book."

ISBN-13: 978-1-335-21321-1

Kidnapped for Her Secret

Copyright © 2025 by Lela May Wight

All rights reserved. No part of this book may be used or reproduced in any manner whatsoever without written permission.

Without limiting the author's and publisher's exclusive rights, any unauthorized use of this publication to train generative artificial intelligence (AI) technologies is expressly prohibited.

This is a work of fiction. Names, characters, places and incidents are either the product of the author's imagination or are used fictitiously. Any resemblance to actual persons, living or dead, businesses, companies, events or locales is entirely coincidental.

For questions and comments about the quality of this book, please contact us at CustomerService@Harlequin.com.

TM and ® are trademarks of Harlequin Enterprises ULC.

 Harlequin Enterprises ULC
22 Adelaide St. West, 41st Floor
Toronto, Ontario M5H 4E3, Canada
www.Harlequin.com

Printed in Lithuania

KIDNAPPED
FOR HER SECRET

CHAPTER ONE

IN A ROOM full of eyes watching her, only *his* made Aurora Arundel feel like an impostor.

She was projecting, she knew. She shouldn't be in New York. Not for this exclusive auction of a single piece of coveted artwork, or for the masquerade ball that followed.

It wasn't her invitation. It had been meant for her parents. But the dead couldn't forbid her from attending tonight.

The dead couldn't complain that she'd stolen their invitation.

Only she knew that the gold embossed invitation wasn't hers as she moved through the black iron gates and up the pebbled driveway to the columned entrance of Eachus House. Only she noticed her fingers trembling as she released the invitation from her sapphire-adorned fingers into the white-gloved hands of the man who stood beneath the cherub-topped entrance.

The prayer on her lips had been for her ears only, thanking whatever gods that be that she was able to keep her spine straight and her head held high as she was ushered her through the heavy oak doors and guided through hallways with painted ceilings and ornate walls, up the floating oak staircase, and finally to the green drawing room, transformed, only for tonight, only for the invited, into an auction room.

Gilded mirrors lined the vivid green walls. The velvet apple-green drapes were drawn against the night. An oak lectern displaying the name of a famous auction house was positioned in front of a marble fireplace of epic proportions, masterfully crafted with silver-accented winding vines.

Ball gown after ball gown moved around the room as everyone began to take their seats. Aurora had been handed a gold-etched paddle, and the auctioneer had taken her to her seat in front of a podium, where the wooden legs of the easel beside her peeked out from beneath a black cloth.

The room was heavy with tension. All eyes fastened on the easel's black cloth. All hands itched to reveal what lay beneath.

This was the appetiser for the night before the red ballroom opened its doors and they were all encouraged to indulge in champagne, music and the discretion their masks would afford them for the night.

Only the staff knew who was behind the masks, and only because they knew the names allotted to the numbered paddles.

And Aurora understood it to be one of those games the elite played. The night would start this way in order to build the anticipation, to fire the blood—*to heat it*.

The rich didn't care that tonight was supposed to be for charity. They didn't care about those the charity would support in their darkest hour.

Her parents had certainly never cared.

But *she* did.

Up and up Aurora drove the bid. The price rising to

hundreds of thousands of dollars within minutes for a painting no one would see until the bidding war was over.

And *his* gaze intensified with every bid she placed.

His tilted head, his elegant, bow-tied neck, arched so he could stare at her from the front row of intricately carved antique white chairs. The curved gold leaf mask covering his cheeks, his nose, and his upper lip only sharpened his green-rimmed irises, making the inner amber of his eyes glow.

She was aware of how different her gown was from all the others around her. Her mother wouldn't have approved of her dress either. The colour or the cut. *The sequins.* How she shimmered under the chandelier hanging from the high ceiling. How it drew attention to her.

Her mother, Lady Arundel, wife of Lord Arundel, most definitely would not have approved of the mask she'd chosen. The dainty pearls rising in stalks from the blue-and-brushed gold mask. The shells clustered on the right-hand side, interlaced with the purest of diamonds and uniquely cut sapphires.

She knew what she looked like. A mermaid. She'd chosen the off-the-shoulder asymmetrical gown with its thigh-high slit to showcase she was, in fact, human, with legs. Each adornment she'd approved. On purpose. Because she liked them. She liked that tonight, she was daring. Uncompromising.

Yet under the onslaught of the man's gaze, the bow on her left shoulder felt too big. Her bare right shoulder felt too exposed. Too naked. She felt too bright. Too colourful. Too breathless.

The bodice of her aquamarine dress felt too tight. And she was all too conscious of the skin and muscle beneath it. Of her breasts tightening, her nipples hardening.

Aurora swallowed, readying herself to continue the bidding. For herself. For her brother.

Pain settled inside her chest. Still acute even after all this time. Still as visceral as the night she'd been told he was gone.

She straightened her spine, squared her shoulders. She would end this. Now. She would win for Michael. For all the times she'd let him down, for all the times she hadn't fought for him.

Her pulse raced. Her heart hammered hard inside her ribs. 'Fifty million,' she said. The crowded room gasped. But he didn't. The eyes holding hers hostage didn't blink.

'Where's fifty million and one?' The rhythmic auctioneer's chant trickled into her consciousness, but her eyes lowered to the subtle movement of his mouth.

Slowly, the pink tip of his tongue revealed itself to sweep across his full, blushed-pink bottom lip. And she felt it. The gentle stroke of his tongue on her.

A gasp leapt out from her parted lips in a hush of expelled air.

'Anyone?' the auctioneer continued from the front of the room.

She waited for the stranger's mouth to move. For him to bid against her.

She wanted to hear his voice, she realised. She wanted to know if it matched the intensity of his gaze. But he didn't speak. The set line of his bearded jaw was a sculpted thing. A *beautiful* thing defined by a thousand chestnut hairs interlaced with strings of red fire, kissed by shards of ice.

'Fifty million, and holding...'

Aurora raised her gaze from his jaw to his eyes to find him still staring at her.

'Are we all done?'

The silence pulsed.

'And selling at fifty million US dollars...' The gavel fell. *'Sold.'*

The stranger looked away, and Aurora released the breath she hadn't known she was holding. Only then did the tightness—*the burn*—in her chest ease. She had won.

He turned his back on her, revealing his chestnut hair speckled with grey, pulled back at his nape in a low bun, sat on the crisp white collar of his shirt.

As he stood, her gaze swept over his magnificent stature. He was a giant. At least six-foot-five. A Viking ripped from an era long ago. His broad shoulders tense with a barely contained energy inside the sculpted fabric of his black tuxedo.

Without another glance in her direction, he walked out of an oak-panelled side door.

And he took the air with him. Stole it.

The room was suddenly too stifling, too thin yet too heavy at the same time. As if he'd ripped something from the very core of her existence—her ability to breathe, to inhale.

Aurora nipped at the inside of her cheek.

She was being ridiculous.

He was no one. Certainly no one she knew. A stranger.

'Thank you for your bids. And congratulations...?'

Aurora turned back to the auctioneer as she spoke and held up her paddle, showing him the number on the front.

'Congratulations, 265.'

The auctioneer, with her unmasked face and her long strands of black silken hair swishing on her shoulders, moved to the easel. She raised her slender brown fingers, her nails painted in a glittering gold, matching her own billowing gown. She gripped the black cloth, and everyone in the room held their breath in anticipation.

'I give you *Divinity*,' she said, and pulled the cloth free.

Applause boomed from everybody in the room.

Aurora settled her gaze on the single piece of artwork she'd won. It was lighted to perfection beside the auctioneer's lectern. The smallest details of the little boy's face, painted in heavy, bold lines in a medium she didn't recognise, were visible, right down to the smallest cluster of freckles on his right cheek. And she realised she knew the artist. Sebastian Shard. She understood his uncouth methods and the use of an assortment of uncommon media had made him a household name, along with his inspirational flight to fame from the streets.

It was a beautiful piece. A haunting piece. Green-and-amber eyes looked out at their audience, asking for something she had seen in her brother's eyes the night he'd begged her parents not to disown him, pleaded for their help, not their disinheritance.

You should have helped him.

A tightness gripped her throat.

She looked over the masked crowd, dressed in their finery, the atmosphere buzzing with an adrenaline she didn't feel. Not yet. But surely she would, wouldn't she?

Tonight, the fifty million dollars she had paid for the piece of artwork before her would be donated to those without shelter, without a home. To those who lived on the streets. It was a cause her parents should have invested in long ago. They should have put aside their ugly views and done the right thing by their son as a way of making amends.

She waited for it. The exhilaration. But nothing came. No relief. Not redemption.

And Aurora began to understand that despite what she'd hoped, this one altruistic act didn't erase all the times she'd let her parents trample her moral consciousness. They never would have listened to her anyway, but she knew her silence went deeper.

Disgust crawled over her skin.

She had so desperately needed their love, their approval...

Golden girl, Michael had christened her, and she'd played her role impeccably. She'd been the perfect daughter, and still they'd withheld the love that should have been unconditional, should have been given to both children freely.

Her chest ached. She knew that tonight didn't redeem her. It wouldn't bring her brother back. Wouldn't stop the guilt she felt for remaining her parents' golden girl while Michael had died the black sheep.

But this was a start, right?

Tonight, she had broken free of their chains and paid an enormous sum to a charity that helped people like her brother. People who didn't have or weren't able to go home.

So why didn't it feel...*good*?

Because you're too late. You can't save him now.

The applause around her died.

And so too did something inside Aurora.

She clenched her hands into tight fists, the heavy handle of the gold paddle biting into her flesh.

What was the point of any of this? The dress? The shoes?

She never should have come here. Tonight meant nothing. Not to her brother. Not really to the people on the streets her money would support. Because this event, the people in this room, her parents, even Aurora herself, were so far removed from what her brother had lived through. What he had died enduring.

Taking a deep, pained breath, she gazed at the flamboyant bodies now being taken into the ballroom. Into a room where they would smile and nod, pleased with themselves for attending an event that would do good for people they would never see, never recognise as human.

In a minute, maybe an hour, they would forget why they had come here. Who tonight *should* be benefiting. They'd forget the people lining in queues to receive a bundle of fresh underwear and blankets so they could huddle, still cold, under a sky that would show them no mercy when the winter came.

A sky that had showed no mercy to Michael.

Did she really think a donation would make it all better? She was no better than any of them.

Aurora dropped the paddle. She needed out. Out of this room.

Blinded by grief and regret, she pushed herself through the crowd and through the doors, hurried along the wood-lined halls, and down the floating staircase. The bow on her hip, too big and obscene, she realised now, caught the vase standing in the alcove at the head of the staircase.

It fell. Smashed in to a thousand pieces of ceramic green. But on she ran without looking back. They could add it to her bill. She didn't care.

Her body urged her to go faster, as fast as her heels would allow. At the bottom of the oak stairs, she unhooked the silver straps around her ankles and slipped her heeled sandals free, one at a time.

Barefoot, she ran through the silk-lined corridor until she came to the first door that led outside.

She yanked down the silver handles and pushed open the French doors. Cool air greeted her flushed skin as she stared up at the starless sky. She dropped her shoes where she stood on the terrace. Eachus House was behind her, the grounds sprawled out before her, a perfectly manicured lawn, with trees on either side blocking out the skyline of New York.

And she did the only thing she could. She kept running.

It didn't matter which way. If she took the stairs leading down to the gardens on the right or the left. It didn't matter that shadows lay at the end of the lawn. It didn't matter that beyond the shadows were two hundred acres of woodlands, ponds, and landscaped meadows. It didn't matter where she went, only that she kept moving. As fast and as far as she could.

The bare soles of her feet tingled from the crush of the damp lawn, but she didn't stop. Not even when the grass turned to stone beneath her feet. She followed the softly lit path, through the man-made tunnel of tall firs, interlaced with swaying weeping willows, until she reached a dead end.

Black iron gates, bracketed by headed stone pillars, barred her way. She reached for the gold square in the centre, the key hole empty, and pushed.

Aurora stepped inside. Into an overgrown walled garden of wild flowers.

The trees outside the gates, and the high brick walls covered in ivy, hid this place from the windows of Eachus House.

The gate creaked as she closed it.

A rebellious mist of grief and guilt pressed down on

her chest. It urged her to release the ugly truth threatening to consume her whole.

Her flesh goose pimpled. She shivered. How cold had her brother been? How scared had he been before the cold took him?

She'd never outrun it. Not her regret. Not her grief. Aurora's guilt was hers to carry forever, because she needed forgiveness from the one person who could never give it to her. She raised her face to the sky and closed her eyes. She wouldn't be worthy of it, even if he'd lived.

What she had done was undeniable. Unforgiveable. For twenty-one years, her silence, her complicity, her fear of standing up to her parents had killed him.

She didn't want to deny the truth anymore. The roar of it, so thick in her throat it was choking her.

Aurora opened her mouth, and she screamed.

Sebastian Shard watched her.

He stood under the domed roof, inside the walled garden, unseen in the shadows of the colonnade, but he saw her nestled in the wild flowers. He heard her. Not the woman who had been in the auction room, but the creature concealed within.

A creature in pain.

A mask of gold, and the perfect shade of oceanic blue, concealed her face and adorned it with shells and pearls of the sea.

She looked like a mermaid. A siren who'd lost her tail. Stranded on land, with two bare feet, coated in moisture and dirt. Her dress clung to her body like a second skin, and she shimmered.

Her elongated neck strained towards the sky. Towards the gods, begging them to hear her song. Calling to those who created her to collect her from where she stood and take her. But they wouldn't hear her. They never did. No matter how raw the prayer. How honest the roar.

The gods had forgotten them all.

He should know. He recognised the sound pulsing in his ears. And the sound unlocked the memory he'd buried deep—reminded him of a time long ago when he'd stood all alone in the dark, begging those same gods to take him too.

It was too intimate, too dangerous to listen to the rasp and curl of her voice, because it moved him. Enough that he stepped out from the shadows and into the soft light.

A dozen hidden lampposts discreetly placed in the foliage hugging the walls lit the space as if they were fireflies herding together inside the plants themselves.

He approached her on silent footfall. His leather shoes were cushioned by the vines spreading across the well-worn path of broken stone.

He did not want to get closer, he told himself.

He didn't want to watch her lips kiss the air.

He did not want to know why she sang to the dark sky.

He wanted her gone. Wanted to be gone from her presence.

But still he moved. Lured in by her siren's call. Its raw and uncensored melody.

He reached her. No more than two feet of distance between them. And she smelled of the night sky and the promise of a reckoning.

She stopped screaming then. But her breath came in short, ragged bursts. Her bodice pulled in tightly with each breath, pushing against her small breasts, making them strain against the fabric.

Black lashes swept upwards to reveal eyes too dark—

too deep. Her eyes flew wide open beneath her mask. *'You!'*

'Me,' he agreed, owning who he was. The man who had stared at her in the auction room. Coveted her youthful grandeur, which reminded him of someone. Wishing she was that someone else. That his sister could take her place and be there with him. In a room of opulence, her every desire, his wish to grant.

She cleared her throat. 'You like to watch?' she asked, her voice a pained husk of too much air spent from her lungs.

'Yes,' he admitted, because he did. It was what he did. His only purpose. To watch, and transcribe what he saw to whatever canvas he had to hand, in whatever medium was closest. And he found no shame in watching her before. Or now.

She gasped. 'And who gave you permission to look?' Her eyes left his and scanned the space they shared.

'Do you not like to be looked at?'

'No.' Her gaze locked back on to his. 'Not the way you look at me.'

He inched closer, pulled by some invisible steel thread. But he resisted. Planted his feet. 'And how do I look at you?' he asked, but he knew the answer.

He knew his anger had been misplaced. *Illogical.* But still, he'd felt it, and she'd known it.

She'd understood his eyes, watching her in the auction room. The determined thrust of her chin, the frivolous wave of her hand as she'd bid on his artwork, had not been complimentary.

His sister would've been older than she clearly was. But his sister would never know the pleasure of waving one's hand and getting the object of her desire simply because she wanted it. She would never sit in a ball gown, or dance in a room full of people who would have once walked past her on the street and ignored her hardships. *Her suffering!*

This woman was not his sister.

Sebastian's sister was dead.

But this woman was alive. Breathing the same air he breathed.

'Like you know,' she whispered.

'Know what?'

'That I don't belong here.'

'You don't,' he agreed. He despised them all, but tonight, he'd despised *her* most. But he'd been wrong. She wasn't one of them. The masked elite who felt no pain or empathy. She was hurting.

'Is it so easy to tell?' she asked. 'So easy to see?'

'It is.' He swallowed. A mistake, because all he could taste was her.

'What gave it away?' She placed her hands on her hips, palms open, and his gaze followed the movement. 'The dress,' she concluded. 'My mother would have hated it, too. She'd never have let me choose it.'

He locked his jaw. He didn't hate it. It was a perfect choice. He liked it far too much.

'I wouldn't be here if she were alive.' Her hands waved at nothing in particular. 'I'd still be in the Cotswolds, smiling and nodding at things that did not make me want to smile.' The muscles in her throat tightened. 'They made me want to—'

'Scream?'

'Yes.' She flushed from the neck up, and he wanted to see beneath the mask. See the heat meet her cheeks and flood it.

'I thought screaming would make me feel better.'

'Did it?' he asked, because it had not made him feel better. It had drained him until he'd collapsed on the street and stayed there for a decade. But she was standing, and that intrigued him.

'It didn't.' She shook her head. The stalk of pearls rising from her mask danced. 'None of it has. Not coming here.' She reached up behind her mask, her fingers fumbling. 'Not this stupid mask!'

'Leave it on,' he commanded, because he would not give in to the temptation to see her face.

'*Why*?' she asked. 'When you can see straight through it? You know who my parents are, don't you? You know what they did? What *I* did?'

Questions he had no right to ask fought to be asked. He did not want to know her. Yet this creature fascinated him. And he couldn't help it. He asked, 'What did you do?'

Her nose twitched beneath her mask. 'I left my brother to die.'

His throat closed. Like he'd left his sister to die, too. Unprotected. Alone.

'I came here,' she continued when he didn't speak. Couldn't speak. 'Hoping, despite my parents' view of homelessness. Their ugly view that those who end up alone and on the streets somehow—' her slender shoulders rose and fell, drawing his attention to her taut collarbone and the hollow in its centre '—deserved it. Like my brother.'

'Your brother?' he asked. 'Was homeless?'

She nodded. 'I thought investing money—their money—would help.' She scraped perfectly white teeth across her bottom lip. 'But it's not enough. It's too late.

My rebellion here, taking a stand against my parents' views on the world means nothing. Not for Michael.' She sucked in air through flaring nostrils. 'He's dead.'

'When did he die?' Sebastian asked. And it was raw in his throat. Not the question, but the similarity of their fates.

He'd donated the art tonight, and all the proceeds would be going back to the community he'd lived with for a decade. But she was right. It wasn't enough. Not for the people on the streets. Not for the dead.

'A year ago,' she confessed. 'And I left him there to die, on the streets, because my parents said it had to be that way. That he couldn't be saved. That they'd tried. But they hadn't tried, not really. They disinherited him. Turned their backs on him. And so did I.' Her slender throat convulsed. 'I… I should have been there for him.' Her black lashes swept down. Shutting him out. 'But I wasn't.'

His stomach dropped.

He hadn't been there for his sister either.

'Why not? Why weren't you there for him?' he asked, echoing the questions he'd asked himself too many times, over too many years, and always his answers were too weak—too selfish.

Her mouth grappled with what to say next.

'Why were you not there for your brother?' he pushed, because he wanted to hear it. Her justification for her failures. He'd never been able to justify his. His guilt was his punishment. A punishment he deserved. And he wanted no parole. No early release. This was his life sentence. To allow himself nothing but the pain, without reprieve.

'I wanted to believe them,' she admitted, and her eyes opened.

'Believe who?'

'My parents. I wanted to believe that their tough love—' she said, the word *love* in inverted commas '—would wake him up, bring him back, the old Michael. But it didn't. It brought him back in a coffin.'

His throat closed. Amelia never had a coffin. She didn't have a grave.

'He'd broken so many promises,' she continued, 'and the night my parents put him out on the streets, I didn't believe him when he said he'd change. I didn't believe *in* him. And I... I...if I'd stood up for him, if I'd sided with him, and he'd broken another promise to my parents, to me... My parents, they would have...' She expelled a heavy breath.

'Your parents would have what?'

'Taken me off the pedestal that they'd put me on,' she confessed. 'They would have kicked it out with both feet and left me on the floor too. And I was scared. I wasn't brave. I'm not brave. I'm still hiding behind this mask, in this hideous dress.'

'It isn't hideous.'

'It's not?'

'No.' He swallowed thickly. 'I don't know who your parents are. I do not know who *you* are. When I said you didn't belong here, I meant here, with me. Because I can't help you,' he said. 'I'm in no position to help you.'

'Who did you lose?' she asked.

He frowned. Was it so obvious?

'Everyone,' he confessed. The word was a heavy thing in his mouth. On his tongue.

'*Everyone*?' she husked.

He wouldn't tell her. He would not unload his burden onto her. The horrible thing he'd done. No. Besides, he'd held it close to his chest, kept it to himself, for so long, he didn't know how to tell it. The fire. The crib. *Amelia.*

'It was a long time ago,' he dismissed, but the words scraped against his throat. 'Twenty-five years ago. Tonight.'

'Does it still hurt?'

'Every day.'

'How do you survive it?'

'You don't,' he said honestly. 'You accept it.'

'Accept it?' she asked, and he heard the frown in her voice.

'You live with it until it becomes as much a part of you as the blood in your veins,' he told her, because her grief was brand new, and his was old. He knew how to navigate it. Whereas she... 'But you never forget. You keep your mask on. You armour yourself against your feelings. You never get attached to anyone again, and you never get hurt again.'

'That's terrible advice.' Her mouth turned down at the edges. 'I don't want to live like that. No one should have to.'

He shrugged. 'My advice stands,' he said. 'What you do with it is your choice.'

She dropped her gaze to her hands knotted at her middle. 'My choice?' she repeated softly. Carefully. 'I've spent my life making the wrong choices.' She swallowed, and his gaze locked to the motion. To the tendons stretching taut in her throat. 'Choices I didn't really want to make, choices my parents wanted me to make. And they made me believe if I made them, they would love me. But they didn't. They didn't love anything but themselves. They only pretended, called their cold presentation of affection, love, because I made myself the pinnacle of goodness—the golden child they only desired to display for public respectability.'

A roar built in Sebastian's chest.

Respectability. It was all the elite cared for in their gated communities, in their sky-high mansions. But it was all a lie, a cover-up, because the rot was already inside their communities, inside their mansions, in the very wood that held up their pretty homes, and yet they ignored it, until it all fell down.

And *she* was a damaged product of their selfishness to maintain a falsity.

Like you.

He stepped back. Heard the vines breaking beneath his feet.

He could not help her.

'Find your shoes and go back inside.'

Her hands dropped to her sides. 'What if I don't want to go back inside?'

The mask on his cheeks dug into his cheekbones. 'It isn't a choice.'

She stepped closer to him. *Too close.*

She stopped and lifted her gaze to his. 'I don't want to go back inside with them,' she said quietly. 'I don't want to stand in a room full of people who don't know me, don't care if I'm hurting.'

'I don't care either,' he told her, because he didn't care. At least, that's what he told himself, was convincing himself of. Not for her bare feet, not for her flesh covered in goose bumps. He did not want to carry her back inside to shelter, to warmth.

'Do you really want to be alone?' she asked. 'On the twenty-fifth anniversary of all you have lost?'

His spine stiffened. 'I do.'

She shook her head. Her high bun of twisted black silk loosened. His fingers itched to release it completely from its knot and watch it tumble to her shoulders. He curled his fingers into fists. 'Go.'

'You shouldn't be alone tonight. And I don't want to be alone,' she admitted. 'I've never had such a frank discussion with anyone. About anything. But we are talking. Connecting. And I—' She looked up at him. 'I don't want it to end.'

'Why would I care what *you* want?'

'If you really wanted to be alone,' she countered softly, 'you would have waited for me to leave without revealing you'd seen me.'

'But I did see you.'

'And here we are.' She inched closer until her scent, her softness, washed over him. 'Together.'

'Geography,' he said dismissively.

'Kiss me,' she said, and it snatched the breath from his lungs.

'Kiss you?'

'One kiss.' Her lips parted slowly, revealing the silken muscle in her mouth. 'And then if you still want to be alone, I'll leave.'

He didn't want to kiss her. And to prove it to his body, his brain, his neck dipped. Until the space between their lips became too close. And he said, 'No.'

'We don't even have to take our masks off.'

'No,' he said again, but the hard edge to his voice was lost.

'I want tonight to be more than a painful memory.' Her breath, warm and sweet, feathered his parted lips. 'I need it to be...*more*.'

He pulled away.

'*Please*,' she said, and the word, rasped from her lips, punched him in the solar plexus.

The gods hadn't heard him twenty-five years ago. But *if*, twenty-five years ago, someone had heard his cries, his plea, the night they'd all died, would he have stood up from his knees and walked out of that alley?

He'd never know. He was too old to change. Too scarred to heal. But she was young. She would know if a connection with a stranger could soothe. Change things for her.

And what was one kiss? There was no harm in giving her that. A little help. A little softness, when her pain was still so new, so raw, and the world beyond tonight offered her nothing but loneliness.

This was not for him, he told himself. It was for her, and for the boy, who had not been given the same kindness.

His hands lifted from his sides, and he pushed the golden edge of his mask upwards with steady fingers. Just enough to reveal his lips.

'One kiss,' Sebastian agreed.

CHAPTER TWO

Aurora's heart raced, but she hesitated to step forward and embrace the electricity charging the small space between them. Embrace *him*.

It was too intimate. Too real. The space between their lips was too far and yet too close.

His mouth was beautiful. It was a mouth made for kissing.

What if she was wrong? What if this didn't make her feel better, either? What if she regretted her boldness? Her awareness of her body, of what it needed in this moment?

But what was one more regret?

She was full of them.

And wouldn't it be worse to have the opportunity to take something she truly wanted when it was within reach, but walk away?

Her gaze lifted to his, and her breath caught. If she balked, if she let doubt in, she'd never know if his kiss was as intense as his voice.

His eyes were not the same as they had been in Eachus House. Somehow, he looked deeper. *Saw more*. And her body liked it. Responded to it and to him. She liked his eyes on hers. Holding them captive with their intensity.

And these feelings inside her were preferable to the pain he'd witnessed her scream into the trees.

She wasn't embarrassed he'd watched her, though. She didn't feel judged. She felt seen. Understood.

She swallowed and then stepped forward, the energy between them turning the air heavy and hot, making all the little hairs stand tall on her body.

It was only a kiss.

It would be fleeting.

She just needed it to ground her. Needed somewhere to channel the electricity coursing through her.

Aurora took in the slope of his gold nose, his uncovered upper lip. Her eyes locked on to the pout of his bottom lip, a stranger's lip that was waiting for her to kiss it.

A stranger she hadn't touched, and who had not touched her. Physically, at least. But he *had* touched her. Reached inside the twisted parts of her and loosened the knots making her lungs burn.

It would be more than a kiss, she knew. She wouldn't lie to herself tonight. His kiss would be the beginning. It would turn this night from a failure into something else, into something more. Something that was only hers. Something she'd chosen because it felt right, and *she* wanted it.

She wanted his lips on hers.

His hand slid to her lower back. He didn't apply pressure. Didn't pull her closer, but waited for her to lean in. Ready to welcome her body against his.

It had to be now. Otherwise, it would be a betrayal to herself, to the woman she wanted to be. A woman who made choices and stuck to her convictions.

A brave woman.

She placed her hands on his shoulders. Used the solid

strength beneath her fingertips to keep herself steady and rose on the balls of her feet.

The tips of her braless breasts brushed against him. Aurora gasped as the touch of him, the feel of him teased her body, made her ache for a firmer, heavier embrace.

Her hands moved to stroke the back of his neck, then moved upwards over his hardened jaw.

She rose as high as she could on tiptoe, tilted her head and offered him her mouth. His hand pressed deeper into the dip at the base of her spine, lifting her slightly to meet him.

Aurora brushed her mouth over his. And it was powerful, intoxicating, the gentleness of it. His mouth on hers.

Aurora felt his breath quicken against her lips.

Her open palms cradled his jaw, and she pressed her mouth to his to finally taste him. To revel in the power, the control, he radiated.

Slowly, she pushed the tip of her tongue into his mouth. Feathered it against the inside of the warm, wet walls.

And he tasted of everything she didn't recognise, couldn't describe, but knew she wanted.

'*Ahh*,' she moaned into his mouth.

And he growled. It vibrated against her chest, inside her mouth.

Deeper she pushed her tongue. And there was his. Firmly it moved against hers. Danced to a tune only the two of them knew. And her body started to ache. Her skin. Her breasts. *Lower*.

Harder she pressed her mouth to his. Needing more. More pressure. More of him. But the lips against hers were unmoving now. His body against hers was rigid steel. Tight. *Wanting*.

She stopped. Opened her eyes. And there were his staring back at her. Vacant. Empty.

Aurora dropped her hand from his face and pulled away. She lowered onto the balls of her feet. His hand, so strong, so wide, fell from her back. And she felt rudderless.

'I've never kissed anyone,' she suddenly had the compulsion to explain. 'There's never been an opportunity. I've never longed for it. Until tonight. Until you.' She realised she was babbling. Overcorrecting a mistake that had made him stop. She wasn't sure what the mistake was, only that she'd made it.

Her skin was too hot. Her chest was too tight.

'Did I—' She inhaled, made her lungs suck in air. 'Did I do it wrong?'

A pulse flicked in the side of his cheek.

She stepped back. Away from the man watching her with an expression she didn't understand.

She swallowed. Took one last look at the masked stranger in the dark who had let her kiss him. And she felt too many things. Not success. Not failure. But something in the middle, where again she stood alone, regret so close to claiming her and this night as a disaster.

'Goodbye,' she said as she turned her back on him.

Fingers, firm but feather-light, caught her wrist. She halted. Turned. Raised her gaze to his. And what it was in his eyes, she didn't know, but it made her gasp with its visceral intensity as he said, 'Stay.'

Sebastian's eyes dropped to where he'd caught her. To where he'd wrapped his fingers around her small, delicate wrist and held her to him. And despite everything, every instinct telling him to let her go…he couldn't.

'Why?' she asked. 'You don't want me here.'

He lifted his eyes, watched her shoulders rise—*stiffen*. And then he met her gaze. Saw the tethered pain. The rejection she felt mirrored there. Something foreign spread over his skin. Something he didn't like.

'You didn't want to kiss me,' she said, and he felt the hurt in her words. 'I'm sorry I made you.'

'You made me do nothing.' He spoke through gritted teeth. 'You asked. Persisted,' he reminded her, reminded himself. 'But I said yes, because I wanted to.'

'The only reason you let me—let me kiss you,' she stuttered in an exhale, 'was because you pitied me. I don't need your pity kisses. I don't need you to pretend you liked it. I might be inexperienced, but even I know a man shouldn't react like that. Shouldn't freeze in response to a woman's touch.'

He could make her hate him, he knew. Make her feel worse. He could give her someone to blame for tonight. Could allow her to blame him for the hangover of regret and loss she'd wake up with tomorrow.

But he couldn't.

'I did like it,' he said, his voice rough, not his own. 'Too much.'

'Liar,' she whispered.

'I do not lie,' he said. It had been his choice to allow the kiss. It had also been his choice to place his hand in the dip at the base of her spine and lift her against him. And he had liked it. The taste of her. The heady moan she had made against him.

He should have let her run off into the night. Watched her as she went. But once upon a time he had been just like her. So alone, with no one to blame but himself for the failures of his mother and his stepfather, the man who was also his mother's pimp.

His stomach roiled. He had only himself to blame for Amelia's death. Only he could carry the burden of that. And this woman was burdened too.

Her load too heavy for someone so young. She was not to blame for the death she'd told him about. Her parents were, for not protecting their child from the drudgery of the streets. From the coldness, the loneliness. When they'd had every opportunity—every privilege—to save him.

'You're doing it right now,' she said, interrupting his thoughts. 'A man who wants to kiss a woman does not react the way you did.'

He swallowed thickly. Felt the drag of his Adam's apple inside his too dry throat. She was wrong. Their whole interaction had been honest. Too honest. He owed her that honesty now.

'I've had many opportunities to kiss...' he began,

'And mine just didn't compare.'

'I have no idea.'

'It was so bad—' she tugged her wrist free '—that there is no basis for comparison?'

He dropped his hands to his sides. Despite every bone in his body that demanded he recapture her, trap her here with him. To soothe her, to change the look of confusion in her eyes and bring back the heated look of pleasure she'd raked over him before.

'I don't need you to pretend. I don't need you to make me feel better,' she said. 'I don't feel better. I feel stupid for thinking—' She exhaled heavily. 'I feel so stupid for thinking I felt a connection to you. That I could have something that was mine, if only for a moment.' She straightened, her spine now ramrod-straight. 'I want to go back to England. I want to—'

'Do you want to know the truth?' he asked. 'Feel it? The truth of my desire?'

Their eyes locked. The silence pulsed for a beat too long.

'Yes,' she breathed.

He took her hand, and she let him claim it. Hers so small, delicate, and his so big, rough.

He didn't know why it was important for him to make her understand she was wanted. But it was. It was a truth he knew she needed. One *he* needed to prove.

He guided her hand towards his groin and released his hold of her.

'You want me to touch you?' she asked. *'There?'*

The length of him hardened even more then, and it stole his breath.

'I understand why you asked me to kiss you,' he said. 'Probably more than you do. And if you touch me, it's not my intention to seduce you, but to show you that you're not stupid, nor are you wrong.' He made himself breathe in and out. *Slowly.* 'I'm just the wrong man for you to kiss.' He straightened, planted his feet and waited.

He did not reach for her hand again. He didn't place her fingers on him. Although he wanted to do just that. Wanted to guide her to him. Instead, he waited for her to place her open palm on the heat of him. To touch him. Intimately.

And softly, tentatively, she did.

She gasped, and he pulsed. Everywhere.

Her eyes flew wide open. She withdrew the heat of her palm instantly. And its loss made the hard length of him ache in ways he'd forgotten were possible.

'My body enjoyed kissing you,' he admitted roughly.

She looked up at him from behind lowered lashes. 'But your brain didn't?' she asked.

'No.'

'So you froze,' she guessed. 'On purpose?'

'Yes.'

Her gaze narrowed. *'Why?'*

'Just because an opportunity arises to kiss someone doesn't mean you should,' he said. 'Kissing involves touching, feeling.'

'And you don't want to feel, do you? Emotionally or physically. You don't want to get attached,' she said, answering her own questions.

He nodded. He'd already told her these things. He didn't need to explain further.

'I made you feel, didn't I?'

He lifted his gaze to her face, to her mouth. And heat flooded him in places he hadn't thought could be heated.

He did not want to *need* her mouth.

But he did.

And the way she looked at him. All too knowing.

Tension flooded his jaw.

She said, 'I made you—'

'*Want*,' he growled. 'And I have wanted nothing, and no one, for longer than you have been alive.'

She frowned. 'You haven't wanted anyone?'

'No.'

'Haven't touched or kissed anyone?'

'No,' he answered. He would have shrugged his shoulders, but his body was so tight, held so rigid. 'I'm a virgin.'

She blinked rapidly. 'You're a virgin?'

'Yes,' he answered. He felt no shame. It had been necessary, was necessary. Besides, he knew the truth of it. His body might be untouched, but his mind had seen far too much, had been broken beyond repair before he'd even hit puberty. 'I'm as inexperienced as you.'

The silence that followed was not unpleasant or pleasant. It was...*thoughtful*. Her eyes were too gentle. She looked at him, and he let her look. He knew she would understand. He was a man with needs. He was inexperienced because he was a man who did not *want* to need such things. He did not want to feel the loss of them. Human contact. Touch. He had made the choice to abstain.

'Why did you come here?' she asked.

'The same reason as you,' he answered. 'To be alone.'

'But why the auction?' she asked. 'Why come here on the anniversary of your family's death?'

He had not told her he had lost his family. He'd said *everyone*. Because it had been. Everyone he'd cared for. Everyone he should have protected. But she knew all the same. Knew it was his own flesh and blood he'd failed, because she recognised in him what lived in her. The effects of severing a blood connection. Specifically with a sibling.

And he knew what it would ultimately do to her. That loss. It would hollow her out. And the fire he saw burn inside her would be extinguished. Her desire to shove all the pain, all the darkness into the night sky and fill that place where the pain had been, with hope, with light, would die inside her.

As it had died inside him.

'Why not here?' he asked.

'You came here so you didn't have to be alone, and you retreated to the gardens when it got too much. When you were surrounded by too many people who wouldn't understand. But I understand. I'm not the wrong person for you to be with tonight. You're not the wrong man for me to…kiss.'

His heart hammered.

'You understand me,' she said. 'And we found each other.'

'To find something means it was lost to you,' he told her harshly. Too harshly. 'I wasn't yours to find. I did not seek you out.'

His brain hiccupped, because he had, hadn't he? Revealed himself to her when he didn't have to?

He could have plugged his ears with his fingers. Shut his eyes. Turned away from the vision, this woman who was like a garden of wild flowers, calling to him, singing his name.

But he hadn't.

'We did not find each other,' he hissed, because she made it sound romantic. As if tonight had happened on purpose. As if their meeting had been fate.

'But we did,' she corrected him.

'This isn't a fairy tale,' he told her. 'This is not destiny.'

'Isn't it?'

A drop of rain fell then, a single splash on her blue-and-gold mask adorned cheek. Would her legs become a tail now as she got wet? Would the rain return her home? His thumb itched to swipe the drop away. To pretend the heavens wouldn't open tonight and take her.

He was too fanciful tonight. Too nostalgic. Too something akin to caring.

He was not himself.

'We are passing ships in the night. Nothing more,' he said, his voice too deep, too breathy, lacking in assurance. Beneath the words rang a question he didn't want to acknowledge, let alone hear the answer to.

He'd make them true. His words. She would not make a liar of him.

'But we haven't passed yet,' she said. 'We are still here, anchored. And tonight could be more than fleeting, for both of us. If we let it be,' she declared.

She teased him with what she held back, with what she *didn't* say.

'Explain,' he said.

He wanted to know why tonight he was here with her, and not face-down, drunk, from the bottles of alcohol he'd taken from a passing server and placed next to the stone bench inside the colonnade. They were untouched.

She knotted her hands, wrung them at her waist. 'We're both virgins,' she said quietly, and again the blush took her. Spread across her cheeks.

'What does that have to do with anything?'

'Everything,' she breathed.

She stood tall, all five feet of her, against the silence that hummed between them in this place of walls and weeds.

'I'm your awakening,' she declared. 'And you are mine.'

Laughter spilt from his lips. It was not to mock her, but himself, and the thoughts this creature took from his mind without his permission. Because so close were her words to what he knew she was now. A creature sent to taunt him tonight with all he'd denied himself for twenty-five years.

His laughter stopped. 'I am not asleep,' he said, but he questioned if he was. If this was a nightmare. If his mind had conjured her for him. To punish him.

'And neither am I,' she said, teasing him with the reality of her. Teasing him with all that was within reach. Connection. Understanding.

His heart stopped. 'I am not your awakening either.'

'But you are, don't you see?'

'No,' he said. He didn't want to see. 'You have mistaken a small kindest for more than it is. You misunderstand...*me*.'

'Make love to me,' she said, and her words were too loud. They boomed in his ears and echoed there until all he could hear was her on repeat.

'Let me make love to you,' she said, her voice so strong, so tempting.

'You,' he accused, 'have heard nothing I have said.'

'I've heard everything.' She placed her small hand on her chest. 'I know you've denied yourself everything.'

She moved closer, on silent feet, to stand in front of him. And his body recognised the shape of her. The heat of her. And it responded without his permission. It hardened again.

'You don't have to deny yourself me,' she said.

His body hummed. Temptation parted his lips, readying themselves for a kiss. For her.

He'd never touched a woman. He'd been attracted to others, but not so breathlessly. Never had a woman made him ache with a need to touch. To be touched.

What would it feel like to claim this night? To let his guard down and forget all that came before it?

She began to raise her hands, and he braced himself for her touch. A touch he wanted more than air, he realised. More than any need to keep his vow...

Her palm cupped his cheek, and he couldn't help it. He leaned into it. Into her. And she was so soft. So warm.

Her hand moved. Her fingers stroked over the hair above his ears. And now her touch was too gentle. Too light.

He needed...*more*.

'Let me take it off.' Her fingers played with the string tying his mask in place.

He caught her wrist. 'No,' he rasped. 'I don't want to know your face, and I don't want you to know mine.' Here in the garden, masked, they were equal.

They were both inexperienced. Both alone and full of grief. But if he removed her mask, if she removed his, she'd know who he was. Despite his achievements, he was still the boy who had grown up on the streets.

'Okay. We'll leave them on,' she promised.

He released her wrist, and it fell weightlessly to her side. 'If we do this...' he started, and stopped.

He hadn't been a *we* for so long, it felt strange to let it roll off his tongue.

'If *we* do this?' she repeated, each word licking at his skin.

'It will only be this once,' he told her, because she needed to understand the rules.

'No names, no attachments,' he continued. 'I don't want a long-term lover. I don't want to care for anything or anyone. I will forever live my life alone. I won't care for you. Ever.'

Her big brown eyes locked onto his, and he knew he was lost to the night, to her, when she said, 'Only tonight. Only once.'

He was seduced. Lulled to his demise by a siren.

You are a fanciful idiot.

She had seduced him. This woman. With her plum lips. Her words. The song she sang, and he understood.

She'd made him a liar, and there was nothing he could do about it.

She made him need. Ache with it.

He lowered his head, and he accepted that this time, their kiss…

It was for him.

CHAPTER THREE

EXCITEMENT FEATHERED OVER Aurora's skin. His mouth was on hers.

And she wanted more. Wanted him to possess her, wanted him to claim her as his. Because she was his. In this stolen moment of time when they'd met, against all odds, both at an impasse in their lives.

The heavens opened.

Without a word, he tore his mouth from hers.

'Come.' He took her hand in his. Fire erupted in her palm, the blaze spreading up through her wrist, her forearm.

Using her other hand to stem the fat dollops of water as they fell onto her from the sky, she moved with him.

'Your feet,' he said as they ran, the rain so heavy it dripped from the flick of his nose.

She glanced down at her unpainted toes, covered in strands of wet grass. 'They're fine,' she said dismissively, but his hand was already releasing hers.

His arms circled her waist, and he lifted. She didn't think, didn't question. She clung to him with her thighs. Wrapped her arms around his long, thick neck. Dipped her head into his throat.

He was warm. Safe.

He strode up the stone path. Pink blooms and white flowers overcrowded by taller green reeds led their way forward.

He entered the terrace between two tall decorated stone columns, a balcony sheltering them from above.

She lifted her face. Met his eyes. His pupils were black disks pushing out the amber and green. She could feel his hammering heart. It mirrored hers.

She didn't need to remove his mask, know his face, or kiss his eyelids, the nose hidden to her, or his cheekbones. She recognised it by the feeling inside her.

It was *want*. The flare of desire burst inside her. In her chest. Her breasts, her nipples, hardened against the solid wall of his chest.

'Are you okay?' he asked.

'Yes.' She nodded.

She reached up to his face, and the air stilled. As did her heart. She tilted her neck, and he lowered his head. Lips met, mouths opened, and tongues mingled. Breathlessly.

How could he have wanted to deny himself, her, this? This connection between them.

It was more than skin-deep. It was fate. This awakening. Their awakening to the flesh. To feelings. To more…

Aurora didn't know exactly who she was, who she was becoming in this moment, but she knew who she didn't want to be anymore. A pinnacle of goodness. A golden girl.

Tomorrow, she knew, she would be changed.

Brand new.

Brave.

'Wait,' he said into her mouth, pulling away from her.

She followed him with her lips. *'Don't stop!'*

'I'm not,' he assured her, and his words, laced with tension, shook. 'I want to touch you,' he admitted.

She trembled. 'I want that, too.'

His nostrils flared. He stepped backwards until his legs met a stone bench. He lowered himself down, with her astride him.

She gasped as the intimate core of her came into contact with the hard length of him.

'I want *you*,' she said, and it felt powerful to say that. To speak the truth of her desire with words.

He swallowed, and she saw him struggle with the words stuck in his throat.

'I want…you,' he said, his voice a raw admission of desire. Of need. And she claimed it. The power he gave her in return.

He lifted his hand from her waist and stroked the seam of the asymmetrical sequins slashing across her chest. 'I want to taste you.'

And words were lost to her as she nodded. She watched his fingers, caught the slight tremble in them, as he pulled her dress down and revealed her naked breast.

'So beautiful.' His finger traced down her cheek, down the column of her throat, into the dip of her arched collarbone. 'Such smooth skin.'

He wrapped his palm over her breast, massaged.

And she felt beautiful.

'*Yes*!' she exclaimed. She couldn't help it. She tilted her head back. Offered him more of herself. And he didn't deny her. He pressed a kiss to her skin and tasted her.

He licked. He sucked. And the desire inside her built until she began to pant. She pushed her breast harder into his hand. Because it was what she needed.

She rocked instinctively against him. 'Oh…' she

panted, and pressed her thighs together. Brought her core harder against him.

'More,' she demanded.

'*More*?' he asked.

'I want you,' she said, and swallowed, slickened her vocal cords. *'In me.'*

The pulse in his bristled cheek thundered. His mouth opened, but she continued before he spoke. 'I don't want to go slowly. I don't want to wait. I want to feel you. All of you, inside me.'

His eyes turned black. His hands went to her hips. 'Brace yourself on your knees,' he told her, and she did.

Her knees pressed into stone, and she held herself above him. He reached for himself. Undid the silver buckle of his black belt, the button. And then slid down the zip and freed himself.

She gasped.

'If it hurts—if you want me to stop,' he husked, 'I will stop.'

'No,' she breathed. The word powerful on her lips, in the air pulsing between their faces. Their bodies. 'Don't stop.'

She chose this.

She chose *him*.

His hands went to the core of her. Stroked the seam between her thighs and pulled the scrap of material aside. He surged his hips upward, and he met her where she ached. Only the tip of him. The promise of him.

She made herself look at him, into his eyes, knowing it would be the same for him.

That tonight they were both shedding their old selves to have this moment together. Two virgins surrendering their selves to each other. To the desperate need to have this moment that couldn't be replicated. It could not be put on pause. Could not be denied.

They were two damaged souls, cowed by life but unable to hide from this. This honest connection. And it felt good. Almost *too* good.

Aurora understood that afterwards, after they'd taken what they wanted for themselves, she'd have to make her choice, to choose this path on her own. To feel everything the first twenty-one years of her life had denied her.

And she would.

She'd never go back to who she was before him.

'*Now*,' she pleaded. 'Do it now.'

His fingers went to her hips and pressed into her flesh. Into bone. Deeper.

She pushed against his fingers with her hips. Pushed them down. But he held her steady. Held her straddled above the heat, pressing at her core.

The tip of his swollen heat entered her. Slowly.

She would not let herself tense. She wouldn't hold back. But she felt the strain in his body. The pulse of his resistance.

'Is it hurting you?' she asked. She knew there was nothing to hurt him physically. But she felt it. His body expanding beneath her fingers, the bulge of his chest, and she understood his battle was internal.

'No,' he breathed through firmed lips, but she heard the lie.

Her voice as strained as his, she asked, 'Do you want to stop?'

'No.'

'Then don't.'

He thrust up inside her.

'*Ah!*' She threw her head back. It hurt. But it was a

heated pain. She was so full. She shut her eyes against the intensity.

But he was…

Everywhere.

Sebastian knew he was going to come.

He held in the moan in his throat and gritted his teeth.

She was so warm. So soft. So tightly wrapped around him. As if she belonged there, and he belonged inside her. Their fit so perfect…

It was pain. It was pleasure. It was *everything*.

He bit the inside of his cheek. Locked his hips and fought the urge to push decades of denial into her body, without care.

Her eyes opened and found him. And only then did he move her. Lift her hips, ease the pressure sheathing him, promising oblivion, promising ecstasy.

She would find hers first.

He sank back inside her.

'Oh!' She ground her hips into him—clenched harder around him.

He reached between their bodies and pressed his thumb to the swollen nub of her.

Her mouth kissed the air. Sang a song neither of them had heard before. Neither had felt.

He was so hard inside her, it hurt. It wouldn't take long for his body to surrender to her, even if his mind didn't want to. Not yet.

He wanted to see her take her pleasure. Own it all. This night she'd demanded, and he'd given to her. Given her his hands, his mouth, his body. His surrender to fate. To her.

And he'd give her this.

He thrust up again.

Her head fell back. Her throat elongated, and he wanted to bury his face in her neck. Feast on her skin.

'Look at me,' he demanded, because he needed her eyes on him. He would to remember them as she came apart with him inside her.

Her eyes locked onto his. And there was no pain inside them anymore. No confusion. Only want. Only him.

He guided her hips, moved her, until he slid to her entrance and back in. And he concentrated on her eyes, and not on the need to spill himself that was so close to consuming him.

'I'm going to come!' she said, and so was he. But he fought against it. Enraptured, he watched her pleasure mount.

Her mask slipped.

His heart hammered. He should reach for it. Fix it into place. But he couldn't move. If he did, if he changed the angle of his body, he would come too soon.

The mask fell. His breath halted as she came into view. Her face of ebony lines hued in yellow gold. Her small rounded nose, her plum lips, her big brown eyes, wide, shadowed by long black lashes.

Her face was everything he knew it would be.

Hauntingly beautiful.

She clenched so hard around him. He couldn't deny it anymore. His own release.

He growled. A roar so ferocious, his ears ached. He couldn't spill himself inside her. The risk was too great for both of them. However, much his body demanded he stay where he was.

He lifted her. But the heat of her body, the tightness of it, ripped his release from him. He lifted her higher. Spilt himself away from her on the ground.

Their eyes met, and hers were full of wonder and pleasure.

'I—'

'Shush.' He gathered her close, and she collapsed into his neck. Panting hard. As hard as he was.

He shrugged off his tux jacket and draped it over her shoulders. But his hands went inside to feel her.

He stroked her arched spine, and Sebastian let her softness wash over him. Let his body mould to hers. And oh, how delicate she was. How tenderly his arms held her, stroked her. Soothed her.

He closed his eyes. Pushed his nose into the escaped tendrils of hair resting at her nape.

And he drank her in.

She moved. Braced her hands on his shoulders and lifted her head.

'Again,' she husked, her breathing still erratic. She closed in on his mouth.

He gripped her face. Halted her. Smoothed the pads of his thumbs across her high sculpted cheekbones. Took in the warmth in her cheeks. Her swollen lips. Need overwhelmed him. To taste her again. To be with her again.

He pulled his mouth away. 'No more,' he said, but his body pulsed, seeking her out. He was still hard. Still wanting. It would be so easy to bury himself inside her again. His body was demanding it.

His lips twisted. Had he forgotten everything? He did not need. He should be sated. He should be anything but this.

He watched her eyes shutter. The wonder slip away.

'That's it?' she asked.

He nodded.

She scrambled off his lap and concealed her breast.

He was grateful she did before he could pull her to him again. Bury his still hard flesh inside her body. Break his promise and have her again.

But his hands didn't release her. They guided her hips, steadying her as she found solid ground. Only then did he release her. And his hands ached with the absence of her.

'Thank you,' he rasped, the finality of his dismissal stinging his ears.

Her chest still rising and falling rapidly, she held his gaze. 'Thank you?' Her mouth grappled with what to say next. 'That's all you've got to say?'

He gritted his jaw. Nodded. And he looked away. It hurt. He wanted to learn every line of her face and commit them to memory. But he already had. She was seared into his retinas.

He tucked himself away. Zipped the fly. Fastened the button. Buckled his belt. And only then did he look at her again.

'It's time to go,' he said, and his body rebelled. He'd given her what he'd promised, taken what he'd needed.

A moment's reprieve.

'*Go*?' she repeated.

'Leave,' he told her with a voice too thick, laced heavily with a need he wouldn't recognise. A need to stay in her arms and press his forehead against hers. To listen to the husk of her breathing. To feel it, gentle and hot, feathering his skin.

'But I want to hold you,' she admitted. 'I want to be held.'

He ignored the hurt in her eyes. The confusion.

She was not his to hold.

'No,' he said. 'Once was promised, and it is done. It

is finished. *Leave*,' he said again, and he did not answer the need of his hands to reach for her. To hold her gently.

He was not that man. He might have been, once. But he had nothing to give or to offer now. He didn't need anyone or anything.

He did not need her.

'*Please*,' he begged. 'Leave.'

Something caught in his chest.

He closed his eyes. Shut out what could have been. He shut her out. This creature sent to torture him with her softness. Her courage to change things. He was too old to learn anything new. To change who he'd made himself be. A man who was not gentle. A man who didn't care. A man who would not care now.

And so he did what he'd done for decades. He defaulted to what he knew. He closed down. Because this was too much. She made him feel too much.

She wasn't his to soothe.

She was not his to protect.

He heard her move. The pads of her feet scraping over stone as she did what he'd asked. And only when he heard her no more did he open his eyes. They searched for her, found her at the bottom of the broken stone path. On she ran through the black gates, and out of sight.

He leant forward and claimed her mask. His hands trembled violently.

The rain had taken her back to where she belonged.

Far away from him.

CHAPTER FOUR

Six Months Later...

THE PHONE PULSED in Sebastian's back pocket.

He wiped his hands on his thighs, the Technicolor of paints spreading into hued streaks of black against the dark material.

He withdrew the phone and sighed. He considered ending the call, but it would only ring again, until there was a knock on the front door instead. And if he didn't answer that, she'd climb through an open window or an unlocked door.

He placed the phone to his ear. 'Esther.'

'Have you looked at it yet?' his agent asked. 'I know it was delivered this morning.'

His lips lifted. No small talk. No softening of her irritated tone. Always straight to the point.

'No.'

She huffed, and he imagined her in her glass office in London, the skyscrapers behind her as she sat at her desk, small and formidable, in the largest and tallest art gallery the world had seen.

He'd only been there once, but he remembered the

determined line of her mouth, daring those who entered to defy her.

Sabastian had dared to enter—and refuse her. What felt like a lifetime ago, in his fingerless gloves and woolly hat, he'd walked up to her desk and returned the cheque she'd handed him. He'd slid it, smudged from his dirty fingers, across her antique oak desk with embossed green leather, and walked away.

'Have you looked at *any* of them?' she asked, pulling him back into the present.

He didn't answer. He glanced at the small pile of newspapers stacked in the corner of his studio. Each was paper-clipped with a note from Esther, demanding that he call her once he'd looked at them.

He hadn't looked, and he hadn't called.

His gaze travelled over the walls of his studio. It had seemed the ideal place to work when he'd purchased the castle. The outer wall had crumbled, so he'd restored it, replacing the wall with glass, and now it looked as if nothing stood between him and the Scottish Highlands.

So much light flooded into the dark space. And it taunted him. A light he could never quite catch in the right position to tempt his artist's eye.

Easels sat in every available space, unfinished. The studio was chaos. Every medium he'd tried. Clay, spray foam, paint. He'd even gone out into the moors, walked knee-deep into the lowlands, collected heather and mud to build a sculpture.

Nothing was working.

Nothing *had* worked.

Until he'd gone back to the cheap spray-paint he'd started with, the kind that was so readily available from anywhere. And even then, the work felt old. Something he'd done before. A different picture with the same old media and the same canvas. The same street wall where he'd let himself first be what and who he was.

An artist.

Was he still one when he couldn't work? Couldn't come up with anything new, fresh?

He swallowed thickly. 'I haven't.'

'I know it's you.'

'And if it is?' he asked, walking over to the newspaper on top of the pile and picking it up.

'They've set up specialist teams to track them—to track you down,' she added, ignoring his question, and he snarled. His privacy was his own. They had no right.

'If any more pop up, without me knowing... They will take them before they hit the newspapers,' she continued. 'They will take them before the local councils can tape them off and keep them safe. And even then—' She sighed heavily.

Anger fizzed under his skin. It was for them. The public. The ordinary. The unseen. His work was not for the eyes of the rich.

'What have you done to stop this?' he asked.

'Nothing!' she hissed. 'I can't do anything if you don't tell me where they are.'

He unfolded the newspaper. The clip and Esther's note slid free and tinkled to the bare floorboards.

The front page, and there was his name. *Sebastian Shard or Copycat?*

And there was a map of the United Kingdom on the front cover beneath his name, with every place he'd visited over the last six months circled in bold red. As if he were a criminal.

He guessed he was. Defacing public property was a

crime. But he knew first hand that when the poor didn't have an outlet—a canvas to release the worry—they found a way. As he had. Even though he wasn't poor anymore, even though he was richer than he'd ever dreamed he could be.

Are you worried?

He was not. He hadn't compromised her. He had not put her at risk. He had not been too late. He'd pulled himself free in time.

His body pulsed.

This was not about *her*.

He'd only wished to return to something familiar. To find a way back to what had always come naturally to him. His art. But it had been lost to him. Since that night. Since her.

She'd thrown him into hell. Since he'd put his hands on her, used them in ways he never had before, shouldn't have used them at all, his hands didn't work anymore. Now he was broken.

He'd had no choice but to go back to the streets and do what he hadn't for so long, without a plan or protection for the pieces he'd left behind.

He'd painted a series of creatures. Mythical creatures, like her, throughout the United Kingdom on walls as tall as the castle he lived in, and floors as cracked as the broken stone path she had run down on bare feet. Ran away from him.

You sent her away.

He didn't want to remember her, but every time he closed his eyes, there she was. His siren. Her big brown eyes hurt and confused.

Shame gripped him by the throat and squeezed. He'd

been cruel. Unnecessarily so. She was an innocent, and he'd taken that away from her. Used her and discarded her.

'Are you looking at them now?' Esther guessed. 'Look at today's. Page ten. It's a whole spread.'

He flipped to the pages she was referring to.

'Sebastian, your work is worth millions,' she said. 'And everyone knows it.'

His eyes scanned the corner of the newspaper. Page ten. He held it high in front of him. His stomach dropped. They had found it already and cut the brick from the wall itself from the side of a local convenience store, in the poorest estate he could find.

They'd taken it.

Left a hole in the community where beauty should have shone. He knew how his work made people feel. Knew it made them feel what he couldn't. *Hope.*

'You should have come to me,' she said. 'I could have protected it, protected them all. We could have made it into a spectacle. A treasure hunt for the public. But you didn't come to me. I didn't know where they'd show up. You haven't claimed them as yours, and without your name—'

'They are not mine,' he growled. 'They belong to them, to the people.'

'I know,' she said, and he heard the dip in her voice. A softness he didn't deserve.

He knew she loved him. In a maternal type of way, because she had found him. Discovered him.

Esther had seen him create a sculpture on a street behind the theatre she had been attending one evening. She'd watched him create art from soft spray foam, sculpting it into a face with a penknife.

The only face he'd drawn or made back then. Amelia's. Through his art, she had lived. Survived.

Esther had taken it and sold it. And then she had found him under the bridge, climbed into his tent, forever fearless, given him a cheque and her business card, and left.

He'd returned her cheque the next day and told her he had no use for a slip of paper with numbers on it, however obscene the figure was. He didn't have a bank account. He didn't have ID to cash it. He had little use for her, a woman who thought it her right to take his work. He had not made it for her, or people like her. Then he'd walked away.

The day after, she had come back with a bag full of cash. Real money.

He had refused it, but she had left it anyway. It was his. Payment for his work. And he had stared at it for days.

Of course, he needed the money. But that bag...

His chest tightened at the memory. It had been everything he didn't want. Didn't deserve. But desperately needed.

Esther had come back again a week later. This time with food. She had intrigued him, and so he had let her stay. He'd watched her as she'd placed a meal in front of him. A cheap white takeaway bag filled with hot foil tins. She'd eaten hers beside him, silently, and left.

She did that every day, even though he never ate with her. He simply watched her eat with her little white plastic fork, sitting comfortably inside *his* tent. And he wouldn't have admitted it then, probably not even now, but he had come to crave her company.

On the tenth day, she asked him a question. Several. Why hadn't he touched the money? Why hadn't he used it to move into a hotel or a hostel? But he hadn't answered her questions, any of them. It was not for her to know that he deserved his concrete bed. Except her final question.

She'd asked him who he painted for, if not for people like her. If not for the money.

Sebastian had told her the truth.

He painted for those who needed to see hope—to feel it. He made art for the people who felt invisible.

She'd promised, if he worked with her, she'd help him to bring his art, and the proceeds, to those who needed it.

And so they had begun.

Esther Mahoti, renowned agent, had plucked a homeless nobody from the streets, and he had risen to heights unseen before by any modern-day artist.

'If you're planning to do any more,' she said now, 'I'll protect them.'

And he knew she would. Esther kept her promises. She had every day for fifteen years.

He did not love her. He loved nothing anymore. But he liked her. Respected her.

'I will stop,' he said, and closed the paper.

'Sebastian…'

He heard nothing else.

His gaze locked on the small article on the left-hand side of the front page of the newspaper.

He scanned the blurred photo. Noted the way the beige collar of the woman's coat was turned up. The way her hair was in a high bun, wisps of black having broken free and kissing her cheeks. One hand was raised to tuck them away, her lips thinned, as her eyes stared at the photographer.

His gaze fell to her other hand, pressed to the rounded swell of her stomach bulging beneath the white shirt she wore.

His lungs forgot to inhale.

It was her. The woman who had made him want. Made him ache until he'd forgotten every vow he'd made to himself.

He read the title: *Heiress, Lady Aurora Arundel: pregnant. Who's the father?*

Sebastian closed his eyes.

The flashback that burst in his mind was a physical assault on his senses. His blood heated instantly. The memory was visceral. The scent of her, the softness of her against him, her tightness ripping a short-lived ecstasy from his body.

He opened his eyes and found her picture again. Her big, wide eyes…

Then his blood ran cold.

He was the father.

His mind roared with the truth, the certainty. They had both been virgins. They had not used protection.

Of course, it was possible that he wasn't the father. It had been six months. She could have met someone—

Bile rose in his throat.

He wouldn't, couldn't, think of that. He would not examine how the idea of another's hands on her flesh made him want to rage, made him want to break things.

She was not his, after all.

But the baby inside her…

A memory gripped him by the heart in a tight fist.

How he'd softly stroked Amelia's forehead, tucked the blanket around her small body, kissed her good-night, and closed the door behind him. Turned the key to keep her safe.

Only he hadn't kept her safe.

Death had taken her in his absence.

And now he had a choice to made.

Would she and his child be better off without him?

Had he learnt nothing? That doing things just because he wanted to had consequences. He'd left his sister all alone in a house of depravity to sneak out into the night and paint, and she'd died.

And his selfishness had come at a cost once again. He'd wanted a night, a moment six months ago, with a woman who'd heated his blood. And now she was pregnant, and alone. *His* baby growing inside her.

Maybe.

He had to know for sure. And if she was carrying his child, he wouldn't make the same mistake again. *He couldn't.* He'd protect them. The way he hadn't protected Amelia.

'Esther?' he croaked.

'Have you been listening?'

He ignored her.

'The auction,' he said, and images flooded his mind again, and made his body tighten in ways he swore it never would again.

But he'd keep his promise.

Only once.

This wasn't about her or him.

It was about the baby inside her.

'Eachus House, six months ago,' he growled, and charged out of his studio. 'I want the address of the winning bid. *Now.*'

If he was the father of her baby…

He'd stop at nothing to make sure they were safe.

Pride filled Aurora.

She fingered the green leaves of the cabbage, still wet from the morning downpour. It was so big, so ready. She'd grown nothing before. She'd never been allowed to push her hands into the dirt and dig a hole. Never been allowed to let a little seed flourish into life because she willed it so, and prepared the earth so it could flourish.

But here was the fruit of her labour. Several of them.

'Shall I cut them back, Miss Aurora?' the gardener asked.

She turned to him, looked at the wild bush of holly intertwined with vines of thorns and clusters of black and red fruit behind him.

'Mrs Arundel would be furious I've let them spread so far,' he said, his shears at the ready to take them down to the root.

She placed her hand on the damp, soft grass and pushed herself up from her knees.

'Let me help.' The gardener dropped his shears beside him and stooped toward her.

'I'm okay, Dennis.' She smiled, because she was. For the first time in so long, she was...okay. More than okay. She was flourishing like her little seeds.

Dennis released her elbow.

'Thank you,' she said, and stroked the swell of her stomach.

Together they stood, looking at the wild bush.

'Leave them,' she said.

'Leave them?'

'The holly, the brambles. Build a trellis,' she said. 'We will contain them, but we'll let them grow.'

'A good idea.' He nodded, and his eyes smiled. 'The student becomes the teacher.'

'Hardly!' She chuckled softly. She did that often these days. Laughed, because she could. Because she felt like it. Because it felt good to do so.

'I will build it,' he said. 'Do you want help to get into the house?'

'I'm pregnant, not an invalid,' she rebuked him lightly.

'It will be good to have a young one here.' His eyes moved over the manor standing tall at the edge of the grounds. Arundel Manor. A house, but never a home. At least, it hadn't been before.

'It will,' she agreed.

Dennis smiled. Waving, he left her alone in the garden of cabbages and wild blackberries.

She walked over to the wall of invasive fruit. Pinched the top of a juicy one, picked it. It was almost black. Ready and ripe. And she felt the urge to put it into her mouth, clamp her teeth through it and lick the juice from her fingers. But she knew she shouldn't. Not because her mother would have been appalled, but because it should be washed first.

She was ready to do the hard work. The preparation was done for the life growing inside her.

She gathered her skirt into a mock bowl and stared at the bump she couldn't hide beneath the green cotton. Didn't *want* to hide.

It was her little seed.

Finding out she was pregnant, she'd known she had to take charge of her life, learn how to be independent, live for herself. And so she had. The cook was teaching her how to prepare food, the gardener how to grow food.

It was something primal, she knew, and she embraced it. The need to have the skills to give her baby everything she hadn't. Freedom to dig a hole in the earth.

She reached for another blackberry and dropped it into her skirt. It would stain, *probably*. But she'd bought so many new dresses, dresses with jangly and dangling bits. Dresses her mother would have hated, but *she* adored.

He adored your dress.

She should not think of him.

But she did. Often. Too often.

She remembered in moments like these, when the world felt so right, that it wasn't because of her she'd changed. Not entirely. It was because of him. And she remembered too, late at night, when her hand, her fingers, found their way between her thighs, and she began to crave the fullness she'd felt with him.

He was the reason she had this gift inside her.

A baby.

A baby conceived of her desperation for more.

And now she had more.

A slither of embarrassment heated her cheeks, but she squashed it. The why or the how, it didn't matter anymore. She was pregnant. She was going to be a mother. But she couldn't squash it. Not completely.

Their night, her words, her desperate need to be close to a stranger, were embarrassing. How hard she'd persisted. How he'd discarded her before she'd had chance to catch her breath. When she could still feel him inside her.

Heat gathered in her abdomen as she plucked another berry, pricking her finger as she did so.

She hadn't gone back inside Eachus House that night. She'd run barefoot to the car park and found her driver. She'd given him the shock of his life as she'd climbed inside, sealed herself in the cocoon of the limousine, in a man's jacket, drenched and barefoot.

She had been embarrassed then. And it had taken weeks for her not to cringe at the memory. For her heart to heal from such a devastating rejection. But she had healed. And so had her feet.

She picked more berries. A punnet's worth. That should be enough for a pie, or a crumble. She would ask her cook to show her how. Cooking didn't come naturally to Aurora, but she was getting better.

Aurora walked up the path to the house, bypassing the entrance into the main hall, and opened the French doors to the lounge.

She walked through the doorway, the sheer white silk of the curtains billowing around her as she did.

How she'd liked to pretend when she was younger, hiding behind these very drapes, that they were her veil and she was wearing a wedding dress. That her groom was waiting just beyond. A fanciful notion. She couldn't imagine being tied to another now. Couldn't imagine being held accountable to anyone but herself.

She was alone, and she was content to be so. For her baby. For the family she would make.

'Aurora.'

She swivelled on her heel to the call of her name. Shock wrapped itself around her.

A man stood in front of the fireplace in dark jeans. He wore a long-sleeved black T-shirt, sunglasses nestled in the V-neck, a curl of hair poking out. Then her gaze rose to take him all in. His chestnut hair falling around his shoulders, his thick neck, his green-and-amber eyes. Eyes she knew, intimately.

Recognition flared inside her.

It was *him*.

She gasped. Released her skirts. The blackberries fell to her feet.

'You.'

'Me,' he confirmed.

Her heart hammered in her ears in the deafening beat of a bass drum. 'How did you get in?'

'The door was unlocked,' he stated simply before walking toward her with long, stealthy strides.

She felt the urge to retreat. To run. But Aurora was done running.

She told herself to calm down, to breathe evenly, to stand tall.

He stopped, looked down at her as she turned her face to look up at him. Her heart continued to hammer and her breathing quickened as she remembered all too well how a moment like this had unfolded between them so many months ago.

Heated images stole her breath. But she would not soften under his gaze. She wouldn't let herself remember how good it had felt. She would only let herself remember the hurt of his rejection. Remember how much it still hurt.

A flash of anger burnt in her chest.

Her narrowed gaze returned to his. 'What do you want?'

'The baby, Aurora,' he growled, 'is it mine?'

He knew her name.

Reality returned in swift blows of anxiety. He shouldn't be here. This wasn't part of her plan. She was going to do this alone. Parenthood.

She did not need him.

'The baby is no one's but mine.'

He moved closer until her neck ached from looking up so high. 'Answer me.'

She placed both hands on her stomach. Held it. Protected it.

'Why would you care if it was yours?'

'Because if it is, you should have told me,' he said through gritted teeth. 'You should have found a way to tell me that you are carrying my child.'

She stiffened her spine. 'You made it clear you didn't share your life with anyone,' she reminded him. 'Not even a lover who had only moments ago trembled with the force of everything you shared. You didn't want to share your life for a moment longer than you had to. You didn't care that I needed to be held.'

She noted the way his pulse hammered in his bristled cheek.

'You care for nothing, and no one, remember?'

'I remember,' he answered.

She did too. She remembered everything. The feel of him. How good it was. How beautifully it could have ended between them. How he'd sent her away with her flesh still burning. Her lungs still panting. Her body, her mind, still *needing*.

She'd made the right choice for her baby. To not even attempt to seek him out. To try her best to forget him.

'So why would I tell you I was pregnant?' she asked, wanting to hear his response. Why he thought it was okay to stand here, in her house, asking if he was the father of her child, when he didn't care? 'Why would I think you'd care?' she continued. 'Why would a baby be any different?'

His eyes searched hers. 'So it *is* my child?'

She couldn't lie.

'Yes.'

His eyes dropped to her stomach. 'My baby,' he husked, and placed his hand on her stomach.

The possessive rasp of his voice, his touch, curled

around Aurora. Her body responded to it, wanted to lean into it. Into him.

But why would she do that? He'd only push her away again.

She stepped back, and his hand fell away from her stomach, but his eyes did not leave hers.

'Were you ever going to try and find me?' he asked, his voice a low growl of accusation. 'Have you even tried to figure out who the man was who took your virginity and put a baby inside you?'

'No,' she admitted tightly. She wouldn't let herself feel guilty for her choice. 'I was never going to tell you, even if I could have found you,' she said honestly, and squared her shoulders. But still, she felt so small in front of him. His eyes watching her from up there with all that hair her fingers yearned to touch.

'But now I know.'

She clenched her fists. 'It changes nothing.'

'It changes everything, Aurora.'

She swallowed, trying desperately to moisten her throat. Her name in his mouth did things to her, the way his tongue caressed it so gently, so smoothly.

She shook her head. 'Not for me.'

She wouldn't let it change anything.

She tore her gaze from his, no longer able to stand the intensity.

Looking down, she saw that the blackberries she had been carrying had been crushed. All save a few.

She reached down for a survivor.

'They are ruined,' he said, and then he was on his knees, catching her wrist.

Her heart thundered, but she made herself look up into the face. It was too close to hers.

'Like us?' she accused. 'You…that night…you ruined it.'

'I did,' he admitted, swiping his thumb against the delicate skin on the inside of her wrist. And it zinged.

'Do you think of that night?' She swallowed. 'Do you think of me?'

She watched the heavy drag of his Adam's apple.

She didn't know why she needed to know. But she did.

She wouldn't let herself regret the question. He was here when she thought she'd never see his face again. Never lay eyes on the defined structure of his noble nose, his sculpted cheekbones, sharpened by the lines of his chestnut beard.

Her stomach somersaulted. Her body was taut with too many conflicting emotions.

'I think about that night,' she admitted, filling the too heavy silence. 'I think about you all the time, and…'

'And what?'

Heat bloomed in all the places it shouldn't.

'If you could change it?' Her skin hummed too loudly beneath his gentle, but firm, hold. 'If you could change the way *you* ended us, would you?'

Something flashed in his eyes. And she recognised it. It was need. Want.

She'd imagined all the ways their night could have ended, and she'd longed for every one of those alternative endings. To be taken in his arms. Taken to his bed, where they would have explored each other. She'd craved it. A different end, as she'd lain on her bed feeling rejected. Broken.

'No.' His fingers tightened around her wrist, pinching deeply. 'I wouldn't change it.'

She stood, none too elegantly. 'Why not?' she asked, unable to mask the hurt and vulnerability in her voice.

'There are no redos in life,' he said, and stood tall in one fluid motion. Swallowed the space that surrounded them until there was only him. 'I am not here for a repeat performance. I am here because of the child,' he declared.

Heat flushed her cheeks and spread down her throat. What was wrong with her? Why did she still want a man who obviously did not want her?

Was it pregnancy hormones? Pheromones? Or was it something more basic? Something more primal that flooded her body with a need to be closer to him because the baby inside her was his?

She didn't know the reason, and she didn't want to know.

'The child,' she hissed, 'is growing inside me.' She curled her fingers into her palms until her nails pierced into flesh. 'We are a goddamn package!'

His eyes blazed. 'Then *you* and the baby will come with me. Now.'

The possessive demand made her toes curl. She ignored her traitorous feet.

'No,' she refused. 'We won't.'

'It is no longer a choice.'

'Who do you think you are?' she spat. 'Coming into my home and demanding things from me? I don't even know your name.'

She took in his chin, squared and sculpted with determination.

She did know him, though, she realised.

'At least, I didn't. I know who you are now,' she said.

His soft, pink lips thinned into a colourless line.

She nodded to herself. 'You're Sebastian Shard.'

His gaze narrowed. 'Does knowing who I am change

things?' His lips twisted into something ugly. 'Because I'm rich? Because I'm famous?'

'*I'm* rich,' she countered. 'Probably not as rich as you, but... Of course it changes things.'

'Why? It will not change the facts. You are coming,' he said, his voice low and deep, 'with me.'

'Sebastian,' she tested it, rolled the syllables on her tongue.

Understanding formed in her consciousness.

'You are Sebastian Shard. A man who gives his art freely. A man who donates works worth millions to causes that will help thousands.'

'Knowing public facts about me,' he snarled, 'means nothing.'

'But it does.' She nodded to herself. 'You're the idol of the underdogs. A homeless man turned billionaire. An artist. A...recluse.'

Maybe she understood him a little more now. His actions, his words... He hid himself away from the world. And yet on the anniversary of a death that hurt him still twenty-five years later, he'd sought company and found her.

She'd made him want and need things he'd denied himself for a lifetime.

She remembered the bulge of tension in his body. The moment she'd thought being with her caused him physical pain.

The intensity of their connection had overwhelmed him. So much so that he'd withdrawn from her and retreated into himself. Back into his reclusive life.

But what did it mean? That he was here now when he could have stayed away... And Aurora would never have known who he was. Never have known he was the father of her baby. Did he deserve a chance to prove he could be the father her baby needed? She'd lived most of her life without choices. Could she really deny him that?

'We leave now.' His hands went to her waist, and he drew her in.

Sebastian was unconventional. His arrival, his demands. But a part of her liked it.

Hadn't she sworn to live her life fully? No half measures? Hadn't she vowed to herself, after New York, to accept nothing less than what she wanted?

And she wanted to go with him. Some part of her was pleased he wanted to be a part of her child's life, to be involved. She'd prefer that…

'I'll come with you,' she decided, because he deserved a chance to prove he could be the father their child needed. And if she went with him, it would give her the opportunity to figure out if his determination to be part of his child's life was true.

His hands tightened on her waist. 'It was never a choice, Aurora.' He lifted her, and on silent feet, he carried her out of the door.

Maybe he was right.

Maybe neither of them had a choice in any of this.

Maybe fate had already chosen for them.

CHAPTER FIVE

As THE HELICOPTER flew above the tree line, Sebastian found it. The light that had been lost to him for months.

It was in her eyes.

Aurora, his brain hummed.

The pilot chased the afternoon sun atop the mountains, and Sebastian saw it shimmering in her eyes. There were no shadows lingering in their brown depths anymore. They were bright, and her light flowed through him in waves.

His hands itched to do what they hadn't been able to do for months without being forced. To work. He wanted to map the contours of her face in clay. To sculpt every line and create a version of her he could keep, touch, whenever he felt like it, because he would not touch *her*.

He flattened his palms on his knees. Refused to clench his fingers.

He would control it. These new, and unwanted, impulses that had flooded through him the moment she'd appeared in the doorway of her house, from beneath white silk. Rounded. Vibrant with the seed he'd put inside her. The seed growing now with the swell of him.

Sebastian had not meant to take her. He had not planned to take her in his arms and carry her away from all she'd known. But the confession that she was not over their one-night stand, that she thought about it, about him...

The moment she'd asked him whether he would have changed how their night had ended if he could have, he'd known he would take her.

She was too naive, too vulnerable, with her romantic notions to be alone without him in this cruel and ugly world.

Dispassionate duty. That was all he could give. All he would give to keep them safe.

His home came into view.

'Sebastian.' Eyes wide, she turned from the window and looked at him. 'It's a castle.'

He nodded.

'It's beautiful,' she said.

So was she. She sat regally, suiting her inherited title. Lady Aurora Arundel.

Her brown skin shimmered beneath the loose-fitting green dress. Beads sat in an array of earthy colours on the cuffs and hem of her dress. Sewn in spirals on the seams outlining her body. Her planted feet were buckled in tan block heels. He yearned to remove them.

He wanted to see her feet. Inspect them. The soles that had run barefoot in the dark. To see if she was injured. If she'd healed.

'It is,' he agreed. Every muscle in his body urged him to close the distance between them. Rush to her, place his mouth upon hers, and crush her lips against his.

Control yourself.

Taking the sunglasses hanging from his T-shirt, Sebastian slipped them on.

She turned back to the view, and he watched her take

it all in. The artillery walls. The high turrets. The foreboding black stone walls.

The helicopter descended to the dedicated landing pad just outside the castle walls. The pilot shut off the engine, and the blades slowed.

Sebastian unclipped his seat belt and stood, preparing to reach across and unbuckle her seat belt, too. But she beat him to it. And the movement caused a rush of her warmth, her scent, to hit him square in the nostrils. He felt dizzy at the assault on his senses.

'Ready?' She smiled as she spoke.

He didn't return her smile. He was ready to do his duty. 'I am.'

The pilot opened the door, and she didn't hesitate. She took the pilot's outstretched hand and left Sebastian to catch up to her. Across the low grass, she moved to the gated entrance, ready to receive them.

She stopped when she reached it and shielded her eyes from the sun. Her neck arched upwards, her rounded stomach pressed forward. He wanted to rush to the swell of her. Feel it again. His baby inside her. But he made himself go slow. He wouldn't rush.

Unhurriedly, he walked to her and stopped beside her. He slipped his glasses off and held them out. 'Take these.'

She turned to him, a deep crease knitting her brows 'Why?'

'To shield your eyes from the sun,' he said.

She took them, pushed them onto the bridge of her nose. And he was grateful they blunted the force of her gaze on him.

'How long have you lived here?'

He hadn't expected her curiosity, didn't know quite

what answer to give her. How much he wanted to share. 'Since...*after*,' he said simply, hoping she'd understand.

Her hand fell to her side, and he resisted the urge to take it. To hold it. Show her inside. Bring her into a place he'd invited no one else. Not his pilot. Not Esther. Only him.

He swallowed it down. The thrill tickling across his skin at the idea of being alone with her.

But he would not weaken.

'After your time on the streets?' she asked.

'Yes,' he replied.

'And you chose a castle in the Scottish Highlands?' she asked. 'Far away from any city? Away from people?'

He did not enjoy people. The night they had met, the only night he'd ever attended an event where his work was being sold, Esther had arranged it all. All so that he would be anonymous within the crowd. Would be asked no questions. He didn't like questions. And yet Aurora had asked more than anyone.

He nodded. It felt too intimate to tell her why he'd chosen this place when it had been decrepit and unwanted, its roof leaking with every storm. He didn't want to tell her that he'd hoped rebuilding this place, piece by piece, stone by stone, would fix something in him.

It was restored to its former glory now. Beyond it. But it hadn't fixed him.

'How many staff do you have?' she asked, looking over every grey stone distorted to black with history and age, lined with moss.

'None.'

'*None?* But it's huge.'

'The pantries are stocked monthly,' he said. 'It's all I need.'

'That's not very much,' she said.

'I am a man of little need,' he reminded her. 'I only take what is necessary to survive. To create my art.'

'Why would you live like that?' she asked. 'You're rich?'

'Because I want to,' he answered shortly. His riches allowed him luxuries, he knew. But he used only what he needed. Employed the staff he required as a necessity. And his team on the ground was only himself and his pilot.

'But that will change now you are here,' he assured her. He'd change it for her. The baby. 'I'll employ a team to cater to your and the baby's every physical need.'

What about her other needs? Her wants and desires.

He swallowed thickly.

He would not meet *those* needs.

'A team?' she asked.

'A chef, a cook—whatever else you want, Lady Aurora Arundel.' Her name felt exactly how he knew it would. It crowded his mouth. Heated his blood.

'It's a title, passed down from generation to generation. It has no real meaning anymore.'

'It means everything,' he corrected her. 'A name of nobility. A rich history of wealth and privilege.'

'You can talk.' She chuckled. 'Staff or no staff, you still live in a castle.'

'It was not always so,' he reminded her, and he didn't know why. Why it was important for her to know he was not one of them. The rich. The elite. The privileged. The ignorant.

'I know.' She scraped perfectly white teeth against the lushness of her bottom lip. 'I'm sorry. It must have been so hard for you,' she said. 'Out there.'

'I have known harder.'

'When your family died?'

He stiffened.

She removed her borrowed sunglasses and looked up into his face with wide brown eyes. 'The press never talks about the before.'

'The before?' he croaked. She couldn't know. No one did. No one except Esther ever would. And even she didn't know it all.

'Before your time on the streets,' she clarified.

'There is nothing else for the press to talk about,' he dismissed her tightly. 'There is nothing to know about the...*before*.'

'I'd like to know,' she said.

'There is *nothing* else,' he repeated. 'I am Sebastian Shard. Street artist. Homeless man turned billionaire.' He used the words she'd said to him earlier to sum up who he was in a few sentences that revealed nothing.

'And who are you beneath the headlines?' she asked quietly.

'I am the father of your child. That is all that matters now,' he said, ending this, whatever *this* was, because he didn't want her questions. That part of his life was for no one. It was not a story for Esther to use to increase the worth of his art. It was his story. His burden. And he'd tell no one. Not even Aurora.

Her brown eyes searched his too deeply. 'Do you want to know if it's a boy or a girl?'

His gaze dropped to her stomach. 'Do you know?'

'I do.' Her hands tenderly moved to where his eyes lingered.

The image of a fat fist reaching for his cheek, pudgy fingers touching him with love, hit him squarely in the ribs. A memory of giving love freely in return. Without question. Without exception.

And you left her to die.

Sebastian's throat closed. He shook his head. The sex didn't matter. He looked back up at Aurora.

'Is it healthy?' he asked.

She smiled tightly. '*It's* perfect.'

'That is all I need to know.'

Her mouth firmed. She slipped the glasses back on and moved in front of him. Through the pillared entrance without him. Down the path of earth, until it turned to stone. She didn't stop. She didn't hesitate in her steps. She walked through the stone courtyard and met the stone steps. One step after the other, she took them to stand beneath the arched entrance.

She fingered the black iron handles to the heavy wooden doors. 'In here?' she called behind her.

'Yes,' he called back.

She pushed at the door and stepped inside. She slipped off his glasses and placed them on the small round table holding a basket of long reeds he'd pulled from the ground himself.

Hands knotted at her waist, she turned to him.

His heart hammered. There she stood in his sanctuary on the grey slate floor of the octagonal entrance to his lair. Waiting for him. And she was an array of earthy colours. Her dress. Her skin…

She wasn't scared, was she? But *he* was. Scared of her proximity, and his body's determination to get closer. But still he moved forward. He stepped inside the ruby-red entrance, which was now filled with the scent of her.

A reckoning was coming, he knew. He'd let her inside his home, his sanctuary…

She tilted her head, and he watched the heavy drag of her swallow.

'What now?' she asked.

Sebastian closed the door and turned the key.

He understood what they must do now.

He'd taken her. He'd brought her here. To keep her safe. To protect her from the monsters who lived out there.

And there was only one way to do it.

He'd give Aurora and their child what his mother and his sister had never known.

Commitment.

His commitment to protect her, to become her protector.

'You will stay here, with me.' He turned back to her and met the determined thrust of her chin. 'Forever.'

'Forever?' A chill feathered down Aurora's spine. 'What does that mean?'

'What is it you don't understand?' He stepped closer. The intensity of his eyes pinned her to the spot. 'The definition of *forever* is for all future time,' he said, and the tiny hairs on her body stood to attention. 'For always, you will stay with me, and I will protect you and the baby inside you.'

Her body responded to the possessive statement. To the undeniable truth of what grew inside her. A part of him. But…

She looked at the closed door, at the key still in the lock. All she needed to do was twist it, open it, and walk through it. But *he* had locked it. He wanted to keep her inside with him. *Forever.* And the commitment of his words, the confidence from him that she wouldn't object, that she'd stay with him, *always*, lit a coil of longing inside her to do just that.

She lifted her gaze to his. 'I'm to be your prisoner?' she asked, and her heart raced.

Despite the meaning of the word *prisoner*, her body hummed with the definition her mind conjured for her. It was not of bars and locked doors, but to always be in the presence of a man who looked at her with such power, and made her feel things she shouldn't.

But why shouldn't she?

He was the father of her child.

He was a man proposing forever.

'You are to be the mother of my child,' he countered. 'You are no prisoner.'

She flushed. 'So what do you mean to do with me?'

A pulse tattooed frantically on his cheek. 'I will do my duty to you, and the child.'

She frowned. 'Your duty?'

'I will give you both shelter. I will provide food. I will keep the fires burning. I will keep you both warm, and the cold world outside. I *will* keep you, and the baby I put inside you, safe, by whatever means necessary.'

'I've never been unsafe.'

'In New York, you were reckless.'

'So were you,' she countered. 'But *that* isn't my life. That night was different. It was…'

It flashed in her mind. The night that changed everything. The warmth of him. The hardness. The fullness of him inside her. But also, she remembered the softness of his hand claiming her wrist. She remembered the swipe of his open palm on her spine as she sat astride him, unravelling. The warmth of his jacket, being cocooned in his scent as he draped it over her shoulders.

'Life-altering,' he finished for her.

'Yes.' Heat gathered in her abdomen. 'But I've never been cold, Sebastian. I've always had food,' she told him. 'I have shelter. *Safety.* I can provide all of those things for the baby. On my own. So these things you offer...' She shrugged. 'They mean nothing to me.'

'And yet these things mean *everything*,' he growled, 'to me.'

The image of Michael, all alone under a winter's sky, hungry, cold and alone, kicked Aurora in the ribs.

'Was it so very hard to be without those things?' she asked. 'How did you survive out there? All alone? Without food? Shelter?' She shivered. 'Warmth?'

His eyes deepened with dark shadows. 'How is not important. I'm here.' He dipped a broad shoulder. 'I survived. But I will never allow the hardships of life—' he breathed heavily '—to harm a child of mine.'

And she understood a little of his determination to make sure the baby would never know such hardships.

'I'll never allow those things to harm my child either.'

'How can you protect a child from dangers you can't see?' he countered. 'Dangers you'll never understand because you haven't experienced them?'

'I don't need to experience a fire to understand it's hot,' she responded. 'I don't need to experience falling on a sharp corner to understand it must be baby-proofed.'

'There is more to raising a baby than rounded edges.'

'I know what's important.'

'And what is it, Aurora, that you believe is important?' he asked.

'I'll never let them feel unwanted,' she answered. 'I will never ask them to be anything other than what they are. I will never throw them out simply because they upset or disappoint me. I will not disregard them, throw them away, when they find life hard, or when they make the wrong choices.'

'All these things you tell me are about sentiment and feelings. Feelings won't protect our child.'

'I've been protected all my life,' she summarised. 'Fed. Clothed. Sheltered. And those things weren't—aren't—enough.'

His chest swelled. And she wanted to touch it. The power barely contained beneath the thin fabric moulded to every contoured muscle of his chest.

'But that is all the baby needs.'

'It's not,' she said quietly. 'I've always had those needs met. But I always wanted—needed—more.'

The memory of the last time she'd demanded more was inescapable. She didn't want to escape it. She didn't regret her boldness six months ago, and she wouldn't regret it now.

'And what is it you think this *more* is?'

'I don't know,' she confessed. 'But it isn't dispassionate duty.'

His eyes held hers for a beat too long. 'Love,' he said, and the word *love* was a heavy, dirty thing he spat out of his mouth. 'Will not protect the baby.'

'I didn't mention love.'

'You implied it. But I will never love you,' he said, and it sounded like a threat to his very existence.

'I didn't ask you to love me,' she said, but her heart squeezed as she imagined what it could be like to be loved by a man, loved by *this* man, completely. Unconditionally.

All her life she'd asked for love, begged for it. And where had that gotten her? Playing a part in a family where she was merely a moving mouth, saying all the right words. The words they wanted to hear. No. Never again would she say words that weren't her thoughts. Her feelings. Her truth. Never again would she beg for love. *Ever.*

'Good,' he replied. 'Love isn't a precursor to doing what's needed. Dispassionate duty is all we can rely on.'

She bit her lip. Maybe he was right. She'd loved Michael, and that hadn't been enough to keep him safe from harm. Her need to be loved by her parents had blinded her to the duty she had to her brother.

'Your room is at the end of the corridor,' he informed her, and she understood the negotiations were over. For now. But she needed a minute too. To think, to acclimatise to her new surroundings, her new life.

'The chef will arrive at four, along with your belongings from Arundel Manor.'

Her brows knitted. 'How have you managed that?'

He shrugged. 'I am Sebastian Shard,' he replied without ego.

But who was Sebastian Shard? Who was the man beneath the headlines? Didn't she have a duty to her child to find out? She'd got a glimpse of him in New York, hadn't she? He was a man of empathy. Passion. And today, he was a man of uncompromising duty.

'She'll meet with you and discuss your dietary requirements. A personal maid and a housekeeper will also be at your disposal. Explore the grounds,' he said. 'Make a list of any changes you require or anything you need, and I'll provide it. Any other staff you need that I have overlooked, I'll employ.'

Shame heated her cheeks. He was willing to change his whole life, the way he'd lived inside these walls, for her and their baby.

It was humbling.

Sebastian's life had been hard. He'd lived on the fringes of society looking in. All he knew was how to survive. He'd built walls so high around him that they were endless. But life was about more than survival. She'd lived safely inside too high walls, and still she'd been alone, and sheltered from the life she wanted to live now. One without compromise.

But Sebastian had been alone too, living a life no one should live by choice.

Aurora watched him walk away without a backward glance.

And the truth hit her.

She'd let him take her because she didn't want to be alone.

And he'd locked her inside, because neither did he.

CHAPTER SIX

THE CASTLE WALLS hummed with noises Sebastian had forgotten.

Chatter and whispers of the new staff he'd employed floated into his ears. The drag of unopened boxes slid across floors. The shuffle of feet moving in and out of rooms he hadn't opened in years got louder and louder, until the single definable noises became too loud to distinguish individually.

And the scent of *her* lingered in every corridor. In every room that had remained closed and untouched, she'd opened every door, and parted all the curtains, lifted every dust sheet.

For seven days, he'd watched her invade his home and fill it with…*life*. And it was too bright. Too loud. Too interesting. Because his feet took him closer to the hum.

Closer to *her*.

He knew why he didn't command his feet to stop, to turn around and stay away, keep watching her from a distance. It was because of the compulsion to see her, watch her. And because for two days she'd stayed inside a room, far away from her own bedroom, and claimed it. He wanted to know why she'd locked herself in there and what the noises he could not define were coming from.

On silent feet, he approached the oak door. He stopped outside it, listening. But the noise from within was too soft, too gentle for him to hear right now.

As he reached for the handle, another memory hit him. The memory of a younger him with a smaller hand, reaching for a handle, and opening a door to find his mother.

His chest tightened at the recollection of what he'd found.

He had not looked for his mother again.

He'd stayed in the basement with the others.

He swallowed down the memory of the taste, too real now on his tongue, too hot and bitter. He closed his senses to the past infiltrating his present with the lewd sounds his tiny ears should never have heard. Of sights he never should have seen.

The handle he was holding now was tugged free from his grasp.

The door opened.

And she stole the air in his lungs.

Her plum lips parted to reveal perfectly white squared teeth.

'Sebastian,' she acknowledged, and her smile was too wide, too innocent, to greet a man who had brought her to his castle and then left her to fend for herself.

And yet she'd chosen to stay.

She'd found her way without him anyway. Claimed her place in a world far away from her own and made herself at home.

Would you have let her go if she'd asked?

No.

His gaze lifted from her smiling mouth to her eyes, bright and staring into his.

He'd been right to take her.

She was too small, too delicate, too innocent with her wide eyes and warm smile.

She wouldn't survive without him. She was too sentimental. She was too focused on the things that didn't matter. Feelings. Someone would take advantage of what she offered. Her riches, her softness.

'Aurora,' he said, and her smile spread wider. Even brighter than before.

He didn't smile. He frowned. Did he remember how?

Did you want to remember?

He did not. His face ached at the thought of trying to lift muscles atrophied by inaction.

'What are you doing in there?' he asked, too harshly.

She pushed the door wide. The hem of her blue dress skimmed across her ankles, revealing her naked feet sinking into the thick pile of the cream carpet as she stepped backward.

'Come see,' she said, and her invitation was too warm, too tempting. Never had a door been opened to him so quickly, or had anyone been so eager to invite him inside.

He hesitated. But wasn't that why he was here? To see what had kept her occupied?

He stepped forward and she took another step back until she stood in the centre of a room. He didn't remember ever having set foot inside. And his body urged him to quicken his step.

She spread her arms wide, palms upward. 'What do you think?'

He knew he should lift his gaze to the room she indicated with her gesture. But his eyes locked on her. Her hands moved to her midriff, cradled her bump, her fingers clasped together.

'Well?'

He finally looked around the room.

'It's yellow,' he said, because it was. But not just yellow. The walls were the shades of sunbeams. Hues of deeper yellows and oranges tinged with pink.

She nodded, the black silk loose at her shoulders swishing. 'Gender-neutral.'

His eyes moved over the white units lining the walls, some with shelves, another topped with a spongy mat. A changing mat, he recognised. Just like the one he'd used for Amelia, only the plastic had been split on that one, repaired with duct tape. He ignored the pain that flashed in his chest.

It felt warm, new.

He took in another unit with a small removable bath atop it. And in another corner, there was a rug with colourful shapes, a basket of soft toys.

His chest caved in.

He understood a baby was coming. He understood he was to be a father. But…

He swallowed, trying to loosen the grip of something too tight closing his windpipe. But it didn't help. The hold didn't loosen.

She turned her back on him and walked to the windows to retrieve something.

She turned back to him—her hands outstretched. 'It's so tiny,' she said, indicating the small outfit she held in her hands.

And he could not breathe.

He stepped back, but with each step he took, she followed him.

Her smile fell. 'Are you okay?'

He was not okay, but he nodded, and she nodded once in return.

'They've all been washed now.' She brought the white romper with its silver clasps up to her nose and inhaled. Her chest inflated. Her eyes closed. 'It smells so good.'

His heart, it hammered. The scent of a newborn's head beneath his nose was too visceral in his nostrils. A smell that was undefinable, yet defined by belonging only to the innocent. Innocents like Amelia. He remembered pressing his mouth to her wrinkled forehead as he held her close to whisper, *'Happy birthday.'*

'Do you want to help me fold them?' Aurora asked.

'Help you?' he choked.

He hadn't been asked to help when his mother had been pregnant with Amelia. Life had continued as it always had. There had been no new rompers bought. The hand-me-downs of his siblings were still in drawers. No small baths were readied for Amelia's arrival, when the sink would do just as well. He should know. He'd washed her many times after his mother had placed Amelia in his arms and told him to take her. She hadn't cared his arms were too long and gangly to be confident he could hold her safely. His mother only cared that he held her far away from her. Out of sight.

'The books say you can never have too many changes of clothes,' she said, though he was still lost in the memory of long ago.

She smiled again. But it was smaller. More tentative. 'I have lots to fold away,' she continued, 'in these tiny drawers, for a tiny person.' Her perfectly arched thick dark brows lifted, a request for help.

He looked at the open body suit in her hands. The tiny mittened hands...

It was all too real.

The baby was coming, and his lungs stuttered with the realization that he wasn't ready to meet it.

His eyes lifted to Aurora's watchful gaze.

'Why didn't you ask someone else to do this for you?' he asked.

'There's lots I have asked others to do,' she said. 'I didn't decorate this room or the one at home. I chose the colours, the furniture, and the clothes, and they all arrived and were put into place, prepared by people I'd paid to do it.'

'And so why choose to do this task yourself?' he asked. 'It's menial.'

She dipped her slender shoulder. The tilt of her head fell slightly to the right with her shrug. Her neck elongated, stretching the skin, exposing it to his eyes, and they followed the unconscious sensuality she oozed. The natural fluidity of her body.

'It feels important,' she said.

It was an explosion in his mind, the realization she wanted to fold these things with her small, elegant fingers. She hadn't instructed someone to fold them for her. She didn't abuse her wealth, her privilege, or ignore the need to be prepared.

She didn't care for his wealth either, did she? Not his name or his stardom. And neither did she need his privileges to ease her life.

She only wanted to fold clothes for the baby, and she wanted him to do it with her.

He needed to leave, to turn around and walk away. But she desired him to stay...

His feet felt like lead, but he made his body move towards her. Towards the woman waiting for him, holding the little romper.

His heart raged. Told him to turn around and run from

the reality of her. From the reality of the baby inside her who would soon be here.

But what could be the harm? he asked himself. *Why not lend a hand? Why not help her?*

You tried to help her six months ago, too.

His body pulsed.

He would not *help* her that way again, he told himself, but his body called him a liar. He wanted to. He wanted to reach for the strands of hair kissing her left cheek and push them behind the curve of her ear. He wanted to cup her face, cradle it, and draw her towards him.

His mouth dried. His lips parted.

It would be a reprieve from the conflict in his chest to taste her again, wouldn't it? To lose himself in the heat of her?

He could. How easy it would be to reach for her, and ignore the agony of the past, and possess her mouth. Thrust his tongue between her lips until she moaned into his mouth as she had in the gardens of Eachus House.

He stiffened. Did he not remember? These urges, these impulses would not protect them.

He wouldn't lose himself again.

He would not let himself...*feel*.

'I'll help you,' he said, and forced himself to reach for the romper in her hands instead of her.

'Thank you,' she said, and released the romper to him.

She was right. It was as soft as brushed velvet. Nothing like the over-washed ones handed down to Amelia that were too thin, too worn.

Agony flooded his chest.

But he would not examine his pain in front of her.

He refused to feel it.

He would feel nothing.

***

For a millisecond before the shutters came down, Aurora had seen it written all over his face. Etched into every sculpted bone. *Fear*.

And she understood it.

She had known it.

She turned back to the windows overlooking the green- and autumn-tinged forests and valleys of the highlands. And with the view in front of her, she set about folding.

'Like this,' she said, and reached for a romper from the pile. She folded the arms in first, and then the legs, before putting the two halves together. And his eyes watched every pull and push of her fingers with intent.

She started a new pile in front of the unfolded ones.

'Your turn,' she said, and she didn't know why she felt so breathless as he spread the romper in his hand, flat on the surface beside her, and copied what she'd done. But he did it faster, with the precision of practised hands. As if by rote...

She frowned. Maybe she'd been wrong...

Her eyes lingered on the tightness in his shoulders beneath his black jumper. His thick, corded neck.

No. She wasn't wrong.

She collected another.

Side by side, they folded.

The silence was thick with something domesticated, but somehow it wasn't a task performed for duty. It didn't feel cold.

A closeness, a vulnerability, pulsed in the air between them.

She swallowed. 'I was scared the first time I saw them,' she whispered.

'Saw what?'

'How small they are.'

'The baby's clothes?'

'These suits are so small. So delicate,' she explained.

His hands halted in their task. Only a momentary pause before he continued, but she saw it. And her hands itched to reach for his. Too smooth her fingertips over the veins on the backs.

'Babies come in all sizes,' he said dismissively. 'Why would you be scared of slips of cotton?'

'I've never held a baby.'

He didn't respond.

'It sounds stupid, but when I found out I was pregnant…' She exhaled heavily. 'I was in a such a bubble. The life growing inside me felt so permanent.'

He placed a suit of the palest blue-and-white stripes onto her little pile. 'The baby will be permanent.'

'No.' She bit her lip. 'It's hard to explain,' she said. 'In my head, I knew that my pregnancy would end, but the moment I held that little suit, I laid it on my stomach, trying to imagine—trying to make it make sense that it would be a real baby with needs, Sebastian. And…'

She swallowed down the confession in her throat, not sure she wanted to admit that she'd wanted someone with her when the reality of the baby hit her. But she hadn't had anyone. Her family was dead. Her parents were not like the parents in books or TV shows who rubbed their daughter's back and told her everything would be okay. But she didn't want to be alone anymore, and he didn't have to be either.

'And?' he pressed gently.

'I was scared when I realised the baby would come and I had no experience of something so small, so precious.

But then I remembered I didn't need the experience. I *was* a child once. An unhappy child. And I—'

'Will do things differently?'

'It's all I can do.' She waved at the room she'd readied for their baby. 'My brother and I had a room like this. A nursery. It was a cold room full of disapproving looks. *This* room will never be like the one I shared with Michael, with nannies who did their job. They kept us clean, fed us and kept us quiet.'

She swallowed tightly. 'But my parents, they wouldn't have known where to start if they'd had to change our clothes or give us a bath. We didn't exist in their worlds. We were barely seen, and God forbid we were heard. But I will know where things are, because I'll have put them there myself. I'll know which toy the baby likes to play with in the bath. What their favourite comforter is at bedtime.'

The pulse in his cheek throbbed.

'What I'm saying is,' she started again, realizing she wasn't explaining herself very well, 'it's okay to be scared.'

'What makes you think *I'm* afraid?'

'Because I saw it in your eyes.'

'We are not the same. We have not lived the same lives,' he told her. 'We do not feel the same fear.'

'But you *do* feel it?' she asked.

He didn't respond.

'We could make up the crib together. It will help. The more things I ready for the baby, the more confident I feel,' she explained. 'And I have ducks. Duck comforters, duck sheets. Lots of ducks.'

His gaze narrowed. 'Where is the crib?'

'It hasn't arrived yet, but it should soon.' She waved at

the empty space set aside for the antique one she'd fallen in love with online. 'It will go there.'

'You mean the baby is to sleep in here?' His eyes darkened. 'Away from you?'

'Not initially, but—'

'The baby should be with you at all times. It's your job to watch them. To make sure they sleep on their backs and not their sides. It is your responsibility not to close them in another room and forget them.'

His Adam's apple dragged up and down his throat. He turned on his heel.

'Sebastian?' she called after him. Confused.

'Play with your ducks, Aurora,' he called over his shoulder.

She wouldn't go back to the cold existence of doing what everyone else thought she should be doing. She wouldn't be seen and not heard. She needed no one's approval on how she chose to do things. How she chose to live her life. But—

'Why are you so upset I'm putting a crib in here? It's a nursery!'

'I'm not upset.'

'Then why are you leaving?'

He stopped in the doorway but didn't answer.

It made no sense.

He made no sense to her.

'I don't want to be alone anymore,' she confessed raggedly to his back.

His step faltered.

'You kidnapped me,' she said, standing taller, making her voice clearer. 'You took me from the life I was readying to live with the baby and put me in your world instead.' She moved closer to him. Invaded his space. 'And still I'm alone. Lonely. When you are right there.'

She'd known he needed time initially, as she had, to acclimatise. To settle. And she had settled. She'd opened all the doors, looked in every room, threw off sheets over furniture so beautiful, she'd marvelled it had been hidden, the dust-cloths collecting years of dust.

'I shouldn't have to be alone, Sebastian,' she said, her voice raw, because she knew what she wanted now. What that *more* was that had been so elusive when he'd asked her about it.

She wanted a companion to be by her side through the small tasks and the big ones to come. She wanted to be there for him too... So why not use the time they had before the baby arrived to cultivate something they both so obviously needed?

Friendship.

He turned to face her, his eyes falling to her stomach. 'In time, you will never be alone again.'

'I want *your* time, Sebastian.'

His eyes lifted to hers.

A low hum of heat gathered in her abdomen.

They could be more than friends.

They could be lovers.

She ached for it. His hands on her body. The fullness of him inside her.

A heated shiver licked at her skin.

'Have dinner with me?' she pushed.

His jaw was a throbbing line of stone, and the silence lasted too long.

It was too full, too intense.

'At eight,' he said abruptly, and nodded, a single deep

dip. He walked out the door without a backward glance. Again.

He was as broken as she was, wasn't he? They'd both lost so much.

She wrapped her arms around herself, but still she shivered.

If they couldn't at least be friends…

She'd leave.

CHAPTER SEVEN

SEBASTIAN HADN'T BEEN back inside the nursery.

Aurora's admission of loneliness that day had been too raw to ignore or dismiss.

He'd been lonely in the early years of his self-imposed solitude. Now he was used to it. But she wasn't. And didn't he have a duty to provide some sort of company for her? To make sure she wasn't lonely. At least not until the baby.

He did.

Every evening since that afternoon, he had waited for her in a room he'd never used before she'd arrived. The table had never been set. The ornate chairs and wine-coloured velvet padded seats had never been sat in. But the candles were lit now. And they flickered in a line down the centre of the table in their silver candlesticks.

The clock chimed eight.

The door opened.

Tonight she wore gold. On her skin. In her hair. At her ears in dangling hoops. The material of her dress strained across her breasts. His fingers itched to touch her. To travel down the outline of her body to her waist, where the material flared out, softly caressing the swell of her.

He'd never dressed for dinner before. He usually ate

in his studio. But she dressed for dinner. Made it a spectacle of colours and diamonds that sparkled in the light of all the candles in the room. And she had asked him to make a spectacle of it, too. To make their evening meals together an event. Something to look forward to.

And so he'd agreed. He'd ordered a wardrobe solely for her eyes. And every night he thought of her as he took his clothes off and dressed for her.

He shifted in his seat. Ignored the heat at his back. Tonight, the black iron fireplace was stoked, and it smouldered. Adding a heat he didn't need. He didn't want it lit. But every night, something was added. Changed by her.

Including him.

'Aurora,' he greeted her, his voice a heavy husk he did not recognise.

'Sebastian,' she greeted him.

He dipped his head. But he did not stand at the head of the table. He waited and watched.

Every night, the ritual was the same.

With unadorned fingers, the gold sleeves of her dress kissing her wrists, she collected her plate from the opposite end of the table, picked up her cutlery, and set it down beside him.

'That's better,' she said, and her smile didn't falter as she held his gaze.

Every night, she ordered them to be seated together. And every night he ordered the staff to change it back, only for her to move the place setting herself.

He stood now, pushing back his chair, and moved beside her.

'Is it?' he asked, and pulled out the chair she wasn't supposed to sit in and watched her take it regardless.

'It's perfect,' she said.

He tucked her in. And he didn't hold his tongue. 'Gold is the perfect colour for you.' He swallowed. 'You look beautiful.'

He took his own seat.

Her hand rose. 'I like this,' she said, and stroked the suede of his brown dinner jacket.

He caught her wrist and gently removed her fingers from his body.

How easily she touched him. As if it were a normal thing to do. But it wasn't natural to him. Her touch was anything but casual. His body strained beneath his jacket and open collared white shirt to press against her perfectly manicured fingertips.

'Thank you,' he husked and released her wrist. Trapped his hands on his thighs beneath the table.

'The cot arrived today,' she said. 'Would you like to see it?'

The blood stopped flowing to his vital organs. He hadn't seen a cot since that fateful night he'd settled Amelia, tucked the blanket beneath her chin, kissed her forehead and walked out of the house one last time.

'No,' he replied, and his answer was a weighted thing in his mouth.

Her eyes pleaded with him to continue the conversation she'd left on hold last week. But he'd buried it down deep, and he wouldn't dig it up. His reaction to her putting a cot in the nursery she was preparing for their child had been unfair, he knew.

He would not react now.

He'd known eventually he'd have to see where his baby would sleep. But right now was too much.

He blinked. Broke the intensity of her gaze and looked

down at his plate, zeroing in on the birds painted in a circle onto the plate. He'd never seen these before.

Another Aurora addition. They must be.

He exhaled quietly through his nostrils. The cot meant nothing. He didn't need to see it. He did not want to.

He looked up, and he shuttered his gaze against the probing intensity of hers.

'I would not like to see it,' he said, and the light dimmed in her eyes.

His body revolted, urged him to take the words back, claim her hand where he'd abandoned it on the table and bring it back.

The light in her eyes.

His fingers clenched beneath the table.

'Not yet.'

Aurora felt it. The arrow of space Sebastian had left open for her.

'Tomorrow?' she pressed.

'No,' he said.

'The next day?' she asked, pushing him.

His lips compressed. He shook his head. The chestnut hair swept across his cheek, grazing the collar of his jacket, and she longed to push the hair out of his face, hold his cheeks, and ask him why. Why not yet?

'Then when?' she demanded, but she kept her voice soft, when everything inside her wanted to push him to tell her everything he wouldn't. Why the crib was such a trigger for him...

'Soon,' he promised, and butted her from the entrance to the fortress that he was. He slammed the doors of possibility closed, with her on the outside, looking in. And there was nothing for her to see but the shadows darkening the green in his eyes.

Soon was too long.

She dipped her head. Looked down to the dinner setting she'd moved to be closer to him.

It wasn't close enough.

All week she'd been subtle. Executed her plan to show him small intimacies, show him what their life could become. Sharing nightly meals together was a start, but there was more.

She'd been too subtle, perhaps.

Impatience made her skin tight. Her hands burned with the itch to clench her fists, slam them on the table, and demand to know who had hurt him. To promise she would not do the same. That their baby was coming. Soon. Time wasn't on their side. But she understood that was he needed.

Time.

Time to get used to her being here, in his space. To crave her when she wasn't with him. To look forward to the time when they would meet and she would sit beside him.

The doors to her right opened.

Her neck snapped towards the staff entering the room with the feast she'd asked them to prepare. Delicacies that could be held between two fingers and examined, could tantalise the tongue, the senses. Food fit to be talked about that could induce conversation.

But all week, regardless of her attempts to encourage him, the conversation between them had been one-sided. She wanted in. Into his head. She wanted the same honesty she'd seen the night they'd met. The passion.

She swallowed, looked down at the nested pastry set

before her, layered with flavours and texture and complexity.

The staff left them alone.

'Shall we begin?' he asked.

Aurora looked at the pastry. Picked up her spoon and splatted it open. The layers merged and spread over the plate.

That was what she wanted. To merge with him. To get inside his mind and explore his complexities. His layers.

But he wouldn't let her in.

She dropped her spoon into the mess she'd created.

'I've lost my appetite.' She stood, pushed back the chair with her thighs.

'Aurora…'

And there it was. Every time he said her name, she felt her whole body tighten with the need to feel his breath on her, speaking her name against her skin.

'You must eat,' he said. 'For the baby.'

She scowled, met his gaze, and thrust out her chin. 'The baby is fine.'

'But you're not?' he asked.

Her scowl fell. Did he care? Did he just not know how to do this? Them? Or was he humouring her?

She felt petulant. Impatient. She felt young and restless. And for once she wanted to allow herself to be all those things. To fight against Sebastian's calm exterior. He made her want to be all the things she had never been allowed to be.

She wanted everything, and she wanted it now.

Meeting him, making love to him, carrying their baby inside her, it had all changed her.

He'd changed her. Made her understand, recognise all the moments she'd let go when she could have reached out and claimed them. Made herself heard. Made it meaningful.

For Michael.

For herself.

'I'm fine,' she lied, because regardless of what she wanted, of how she wanted to act in this moment, he needed her to take things slower.

He needed time.

She advanced a step toward him and dipped her head to his ear. His hair whispered across her forehead. And she did what she longed to do. She touched the chestnut silk and pushed the hair behind his ear.

'Good night,' she husked and dipped her head further. Pressed her lips to his bristled cheek and kissed him.

A low moan vibrated in his chest.

She lifted her lips from his cheek, just enough to claim his face and turn it to her. And the long bristles of his beard pricked at her fingers. Made her skin tingle from her fingertips to her gold-sheathed toes.

Their eyes clashed and locked.

His eyes were an amber blaze, and they mirrored the hum in her body demanding she get closer. Taste his lips. His mouth.

She leaned in—

'What are you doing?' he said quietly, but so dangerously it hit her straight in the chest.

She inhaled heavily through lips that trembled. 'Kissing you good-night.'

'Why would you do that?'

Colour heated her cheeks.

'It's what people do.'

He stood—backing away from her. 'It's not what *we* will do.'

'Why not?'

'Aurora,' he warned darkly.

'My parents ate dinner together,' she said. 'They dressed up every night. But we were never allowed to join them. Not when we were younger. It was only when we got older that we were allowed in, and I realised it was all a show.'

He frowned. 'A show?'

'On the outside, they looked like the perfect couple.' She nodded. 'They sat together in the same room, but my parents avoided all meaningful contact. They barely spoke. They avoided the tough discussions that would make them uncomfortable. They never touched. Or kissed. They didn't even sleep in the same room.'

Her gut curdled at the visceral reaction to the memory. The uncomfortableness every time she was in the room with her parents. The silence. The expectation to nod. To smile. To comply with their clipped instructions or their dismissals. But Aurora need to talk. She needed the hard conversations.

'I have put on this show at your request.' His chest deflated as if she'd punched him in the ribs. 'I have done these things. Eaten with you, dressed for dinner to make you comfortable. To prove to you that you won't be alone. I will be beside you through this. Our pregnancy, and the arrival of our child. I have done this to show you what it means to stay with me. I am here for you. Both of you,' he told her.

'I don't want a show,' she said. 'I want no part of a relationship that is nothing more than a shell of respectability. I want nothing lukewarm. I want honesty and warmth. Passion. I want—'

'We are not in a relationship,' he told her.

'But we could be,' she said. 'I want us to do all the things my parents didn't,' she insisted. 'I want us to respect each other. I want us to talk. To touch.' Her gaze slid down the length of the noble nose and halted at his lips. Hairs feathered the softness of his pink mouth. 'To kiss.'

'No.'

'Admit it,' she pushed. 'Admit you enjoy spending time with me. That you think of me all day, waiting for dinner time. I think of you,' she confessed. 'All day. Every day. And I know you like it when we meet here in the evenings.'

She waved her hands around the room, at the flowers she'd made them put in here, the fire she'd insisted on being lit to warm the dark edges.

'You wait for me to sit beside you. You like it when I move my plate and get closer to you,' she told him, admitting what he wouldn't, but she knew. 'You want me closer, so let me get closer, Sebastian. Let me in. Tell me why you don't want to see the crib.'

The pulse in his cheek was an erratic drum, but his mouth remained sealed.

'I don't want to do this alone,' she told him. 'I want to raise our child together. But that means we need to be a team.'

'I will do my duty,' he replied, his tone too neutral, too calm. 'But that's all I have to give, Aurora. My protection.'

Fire flamed inside her ribs. 'I don't need your protection. I have my own money, my own house. If I wanted to, I could employ a team of guards. But I don't want a team of guards. I don't need a security detail. Our baby needs you. I need you.'

She placed a hand on her ever-growing stomach. His

gaze fell to her belly. And she would not examine the expression in his eyes. She needed action from him. Not looks she couldn't decipher, however much they made her long.

It wasn't enough.

'We could be something special, Sebastian, but if we can't at least talk…'

She didn't want to force him.

She wanted him to want this.

And she knew he did. Knew he needed it as desperately as she did. To exploit this connection between them and make their lives together full. For themselves, and for the child in her belly. For the family they could become.

She turned on her heel. Walked out of the room and made herself keep her eyes forward. She wasn't playing games. She'd put her cards on the table. Again.

He wanted her, she knew. She could feel it. All the things she'd offered him freely, he needed. He wanted her to stay. He wanted them to be a family. But he wasn't ready to admit it. She had to give him the time to figure that out on his own.

And so she would.

Aurora walked out on him. And only when she was out of sight did she run to her room, close the door, and throw herself on the bed.

And she wailed.

CHAPTER EIGHT

One Month Later...

SEBASTIAN'S HANDS WERE still broken. No, it was worse. They didn't function anymore. Didn't bend to his will.

He held them out in front of him. His nails covered in the grey clay he'd pushed them into while trying to create something. *Anything.*

He noted the bulge of the veins on the hands he'd always relied on. The muscles he'd overworked and strained in his forearms. He'd pushed them too hard. And they ached. His wrists. His knuckles.

He looked at the monstrosity before him. It was still a lump of clay. Moulded into nothing recognizable with unskilled hands.

His hands.

He pushed his hand into it, flexed his aching fingers and gripped a fistful. He yanked it free and threw it.

It smashed to the floor at the foot of the window. A stream of light from the morning sun caressed its newly flattened form. Teased it with the warmth of what it could become when softened and moulded with care.

He padded across the wooden floor to the window. He stood in the beam of light, raised his head, and begged it to infiltrate his skin. To warm him. But it only teased him, too.

He couldn't be moulded by the heat in her eyes, her words, her fleeting touch. But the temptation of them, of what he could become if he let her in, hummed beneath his skin.

They urged him to say *yes*, to all the things she wanted. All the things he'd never had, and neither had she. The warmth of a family not bound to a narrative of lies. A show performed to hide what was beneath fake smiles and pretty clothes.

He'd never worn pretty clothes for dinner. But his life had been a show for those on the outside. He'd had to lie to keep the veneer of respectability intact. Perhaps if he hadn't lied, hadn't tried so hard to protect himself, protect Amelia, she would still be alive. Twenty-five years later he still felt as though his heart had been cut from his chest. She'd been ripped away from him in an instant. Taken. If he hadn't allowed himself to care, to love her so much, he'd done the unthinkable to keep her safe, maybe she'd still be alive. If he'd taken the emotion out of it. Done his duty.

He'd do his duty now. Guard Aurora, and their child, from afar.

He'd keep them safe.

He opened his eyes, scanned the treetops, the leaves browning with the death of the summer season.

A single leaf fell, and he watched it. Followed it with his eyes.

His heart thundered.

He'd avoided her for days. *Weeks*.

He lifted his hand to his cheek. Where it burned still. It would have been so easy to lie to her that night, to turn his head and accept her offered mouth. To kiss her as she knew he wanted to. Push his tongue between her warm, wet lips and taste her.

And he had wanted to. It was visceral. The reaction of his body.

It was more than want.

It was *need*.

And he could not let himself need her. He wouldn't allow it. However much his body denied his command to stay still, to not react to her—he reacted.

He understood what she wanted. She had been clear, but he could not do it. And so he'd stayed away. Watched her grow from afar. And she'd grown in the weeks she'd been here. The baby inside her bigger. Almost here. Almost real.

His breath caught.

And there she was now, in the undergrowth beneath the window he was looking out of. *Real*.

He wanted air—wanted to breathe her air. His fist clenched, demanding he smash through the foot-thick glass and reach for her.

Her black hair hung loose on her shoulders, whispered across her bare arms. With one hand splayed forward in case she needed it for balance, her other hand held the swell of her beneath her thin cotton dress. And it was barely there. The dress. Its burnt amber tones sat on her brown skin as if it were part of her. A perfect colour match.

She took a step. Lifted her bare foot, and he saw what was on the ground beneath her.

Instinctually he reached into his back pocket. Gripped his mobile, opened the camera app and aimed it at her.

Her toes made contact first. Softly they pressed down

on the dandelion. The only one in a field of green. The white feathered wishes separated from the flower. They flew up all around her. And he couldn't stop. He took shot after shot. Programmed to capture bursts of inspiration where he saw it.

And he saw it now.

He saw her.

Her hands lifted and played with a hundred wishes surrounding her. Her hands were delicate. Smooth.

She was young. Too young for him. He knew that. And yet he had risked everything for her. Now everything had changed. *She* changed daily with the consequences of his choice to let his guard down.

He never should have done so.

But how could he regret it when she bloomed so vibrantly with the life inside her?

The life he had put there. Inside her body.

She caught a wish. Closed her fingers gently around it and brought it to her lips. They moved, whispering words he couldn't hear, and then she let it go. Allowed her wish to fly.

He could not make her wishes come true.

He could not be the man she wanted.

He was not ready to try. He didn't want to try. He didn't know how to do as she asked and not let himself get attached.

Brown eyes framed by long lashes looked up.

And she saw him, too.

Everything tightened. Every muscle jerked under the restraint of his will to not move. To not break through the glass.

He dipped his head. Acknowledged her. And then stepped back. Away from her. Until the shadows hid him from her. Hid her from him. He turned his back to the view, the only view his eyes wanted to see, and pushed his phone into his pocket.

He walked into the centre of the room. Far away from temptation. From the window. He closed his eyes and stood there. Paralysed. For only the gods knew for how long. Minutes. Hours.

His skin hummed and tingled. His mind reeled with incoherent thoughts. His body felt empty, malnourished. Deprived of her.

He'd missed her, he knew. Missed having her close. He thought of her every minute of every day…

He thrust his hands into his hair and dragged it back away from his face.

What the hell was happening to him?

He closed his eyes more tightly. Commanded his brain to tell his body to breathe deeply. In and out. But still his heart hammered. Still his body ached.

'So this is where you've been hiding?'

His eyes flew open. Found the source of the question. Of the voice.

'Aurora.'

She rested against the door frame casually, her breasts rising and falling with each breath.

His eyes fell lower to her feet, her ankles.

'Why do you refuse to wear shoes?' he asked.

'I like the feel of the earth beneath my feet,' she said without reaction to his reproach, and she moved into the room.

'So, have you?' she asked, as she cast her eyes around the room. To the art unseen by all but him.

'Have I what?'

Her head snapped forward, and she halted. 'Have you been hiding?' she repeated. 'From me?'

They both knew he had been, but Sebastian shrugged, feigning a nonchalance he didn't feel.

'Have you been searching for me?' he asked, because he could not stop the question.

'The castle has many rooms,' she answered, and looked again at the walls. To the art. 'And I have been in every one.'

'And now you have found me.'

'Yes,' she acknowledged, but she didn't glance at him. Did not smile in victory. 'And here you are in the tallest tower, in the highest room.'

'You should not have come up all those stairs,' he said. The image of her, heavy with his child, ascending the spiralling stone staircase, so narrow, so dangerous, made his blood turn molten.

'But I did,' she dismissed his concern softly.

He couldn't protect her, not even from the stairs. From putting herself in unnecessary danger. Because she didn't see the risk with her naive eyes. She did not understand it was a risk to be here. With him.

Like that night?

He hardened everywhere he shouldn't.

'None of the rest of the rooms are like this,' she said. 'This room feels like you.'

'And none of the others did?'

'No.' She reached up, splayed her fingers and let them hover above a face in the picture frame. And then she moved again. Her footfalls slow, the heels of her bare soles making contact first, and then her toes. Tiny and perfect, unscarred toes.

His breath snagged. 'And what do I feel like?' he asked, his voice gruff. Low.

Her fingers feathered one of the hooded floor-length fur coats he wore in winter on the moors. They hung on antlers he'd found in the forest, and they came out of the brick as if they were part of it now. Belonged there.

She stroked the coat, caressed it, allowed the brown fur to move through the spaces between her fingers. She turned to him. And she stole the minimal air he had in his lungs.

'You feel endless.'

'Endless?'

'You are a fortress,' she explained. 'You have lots of doors. Some are open. Some let people inside, but they are not where you live.'

She continued to walk, circled him like a predator, until she came to the window. She turned to him, and he faced her.

The light danced in the wisps of her hair. It kissed her skin. It made her shimmer. Like a goddess in the sun. She extended her arms wide.

'But I've found it,' she said.

'Found what?'

'The heart of you,' she said, gesturing to the walls, to the clay, to the splodge splattered on the floor at her feet. 'This is where you live.' She dropped her hand to her sides slowly. Gracefully. 'Your art... It—this—is your heart.'

'There is no heart here anymore,' he growled.

'It's everywhere,' she corrected him.

He looked at the studio. Tried to see it through her eyes. How the space looked active and alive with unfinished thoughts. The art on the walls was from long ago. A time when he'd accepted his art was all he was. All he had to give. But now...unfinished pieces littered every corner. The mound of clay he couldn't sculpt mocked him from its spot on the floor.

He turned to her. And there she waited for him to respond. Silently she stood in his space. With her naivety. Because so naive was she, she'd stumbled on the truth. His art was how he breathed. It was his life. How he gave back to those who were forgotten.

And she'd taken it from him.

He held out his clay-covered hands to her because he wanted her to see. *To know*.

'My hands are broken.'

Her lips parted, her eyes dropping to his hands. 'What do you mean, they're broken?'

'They do not work.'

She stepped closer. The pads of her naked feet warned him to move away. To drop his hands. But he couldn't. He was rooted to the spot.

'Why not?' she asked, and he saw her hands rise, saw them inch towards his, raised between them. Softly she took each of his hands in hers. She smoothed the clean pads of her thumbs over his dirty knuckles.

And it was everything. Softness, he knew he didn't deserve. But knew he had missed it. The feel of her on him, her touch, having her close, it was everything he had missed every day she had been here. Every day she had been away from him.

'Aurora...' He tried to tug his hands away.

She held on, drew his hands closer, until they hovered above the baby inside her.

'Let me see,' she said.

Her eyes moved over his clay-covered knuckles. And he let her look.

She took his right hand, turned it over, gently ran the tips of her fingers over his palm.

It was agony.

It was pleasure.

It was everything he should not allow himself to be feeling. But he couldn't pull away. He did not *want* to.

She took his left hand and did the same, and the trembling in his core changed. It burst inside his veins. His adrenaline spiked, flooded his chest.

'Come with me,' she said, and then she was leading him by the hand across the wooden floor, their bare feet padding in unison, toward the deep porcelain sink on the far left wall.

And he let her lead him there. Because he could not speak. He could not breathe for the fire eating his flesh alive from the inside out.

'Here.' She twisted the tap, but still she held his hand. Still she held on to him as the water gushed into the sink.

She reached for the soap on the waterlogged dish and placed it in his palm. And then she reached for his other hand and put it on the top of the soap.

And then...

He could not breathe.

She closed her hands over his, wrapped them in her much smaller ones. She pulled their joined hands beneath the water and slid them together. Lathered the soap and worked the suds between his fingers.

Aurora cleaned him. His hands. His knuckles. His skin.

And his lungs squeezed. Until nothing remained. Never had anyone cleaned him. Never had anyone wiped away the dirt from his skin. Even when he was younger, as young as he could remember, he had cared for himself. And when Amelia had arrived, he had cared for her.

But no one. not even his mother, had taken care of him.

'There,' she said, and turned off the tap, pulled his dripping hands closer. 'They're not broken. They were just dirty.'

She looked around the sink's edge. Looking for what, he did not know, and did not have the words to ask. He was rendered speechless by her naive assumption the dirt on his skin didn't go beyond the surface.

'It's more than that,' he said eventually.

She lifted the loose fabric at her waist and patted at his hands dry.

'More than what?' she asked.

'It's more than dirt. The reason they won't work,' he admitted.

Her dress, crumpled with moisture, fell back down to her thighs. She raised her head, looked up into his face with her brown eyes and asked, 'Then what is it?' Her brow creased. Lines deepened in her smooth, flawless skin. 'Why do your hands not work?'

He didn't deserve her concern. Her kindness.

'Tell me,' she urged. 'Why do you think your hands are broken?'

She'd always been honest with him. Since their very first meeting in New York. In her home. Here.

She slammed her truth against him, without apology, every time she could.

He'd offer her the same now.

'Because of you.'

Aurora saw it. Felt it. How hard it was for him admit.

'Because of me?' she repeated.

'I—' His body strained. Every muscle beneath his cream clay-covered T-shirt buzzed with a restrained energy. 'I haven't...'

He swallowed thickly. And she swallowed, too. Knowing this time she wouldn't get it wrong. She wouldn't demand. She wouldn't push him too hard, too fast, until he thought there was no other choice but to retreat.

'You haven't what?' She let her fingers press into his skin and clasped his hands gently between them.

'Since New York, since you, I have made nothing new.' His hands tensed in hers, and she saw the fight he had with himself not to close them into fists. 'My hands, they will not let me. They refuse me.'

'I saw your work in the paper.' She frowned. 'Wasn't that after...me?'

'That was not new.' He shook his head. His hair glided against the strained muscles in his throat. Over the pulse hammering there. 'It was nothing but a stencil of something I had created before. It was paint by numbers.'

'It was beautiful.'

The pulse hammered in his bristled jaw. 'You do not understand.'

'I don't.' She shook her head. 'I'm not an artist. So tell me. Explain it to me,' she said, and waited for the doors to close. To shut her out.

They didn't.

'Since I touched you...' he breathed, and she felt the heaviness of it. His exhale. His confession. 'My hands do not work the same. They do not *feel* the same.'

Her heart raced. But she kept her lips sealed. Waited. For him.

'I have tried everything,' he rasped. 'All my life, my hands...they are everything. They are what I am. All I have to give. But they do not feel right, Aurora. And I cannot fix them.'

They both looked down at his hands. To the source of his pain.

'You are more than your hands,' she breathed.

'*I am not*!' he roared. The pain in each word ricocheted through her chest until it landed inside her heart. And she hurt for him. Desperately.

And she did what she knew she shouldn't. She brought his hand to her mouth and kissed his knuckles.

'Aurora...' he husked deeply. But he didn't tell her to stop, so she didn't. She did the same to his other hand. Kissed each knuckle, each joint that wouldn't work for him the way he wanted them to. The way he knew they used to work.

She was no artist. But she was human. A woman who had to learn to change, to adapt, to her growing body. To teach her mind to think differently, to react differently, because she had changed, *was* changing, physically, emotionally, all the time...

She raised her eyes to his and said the only thing she could.

'If they do not work the same, if your hands do not *feel* the same,' she said, 'then they are changed, Sebastian. Listen to them.'

'They are not changed,' he said, rejected her idea. 'They are my hands. The same hands I have always had for forty years. I will always have them, as they are.'

'No,' she replied. 'New York, it happened to us both. I'm changed because of it.' Her gaze dropped to his lips. 'I am changed because of you. Perhaps you are changed because of me, too.'

'It is not the same,' he said. 'You are pregnant.'

'I'm not talking about the baby.' She released his right hand. 'I'm talking about in here,' she said, and brought his left hand to her chest. She held it flat against the drum of her heart.

'After...after we were together,' she continued. 'I knew I could never go back. I could never go back to the Aurora who said "please" and "thank you" for all the things I didn't want. I would never again hold my tongue in fear of offending someone else with my opinion. Or be someone I'm not.

'I listened to my body—to my mind,' she continued, wanting him to understand he wasn't broken. He was never broken. He was changing. 'I let the changes happen. I am letting them happen right now, here, with you.'

'I do not want to change. I can't.'

'You can.'

'No. I can't.' He pulled his hand from her chest, and she felt hollow without it. Her skin, her breasts ached for his touch.

But she let him go. She let him retreat.

'I'll call someone to escort you back down the tower staircase.'

'I'm not going anywhere!' she said. She wouldn't leave. Not yet.

'Fine. *I* will take you down myself,' he said.

'I won't let you send me away again,' she said. Even though his need to see her safe, the fact he cared about her, touched her deeply.

'Talk to me,' she urged. 'Tell me, why? Why won't you embrace change? Your body wants it. Your hands need it,' she told him, a tremble taking hold of her core. She suppressed it.

'I won't let it happen,' he said. 'I will not change. Not for my hands. Not for you.'

'Why is it so difficult for you to spend time with me?' she asked, forgetting everything she'd promised herself she wouldn't do, forgetting the pep talk she'd given herself about not pushing him too hard. But he needed to be pushed. 'Why do you keep fighting my attempts to build a bond between us? Why are you fighting the chemistry between us? You don't have to.'

'I do,' he growled, not with just his chest but his whole body.

'Because you don't want to get hurt again,' she concluded for him. 'Because your family died? People die, Sebastian. My brother and my parents are dead. Death doesn't mean you have to push people away. You don't have to push me away.'

His chest swelled. 'But I must,' he said roughly, and his fists clenched at his sides. His body turning into solid, immovable stone.

'Why?'

His nostrils flared. His jaw squared.

'Tell me,' she pleaded. 'Make me understand why you can't let us be what I know we could. Together, in all the ways couples can be together. Why are you fighting this so hard?'

And she fought with every fibre of her being not to lean into him. To keep her distance.

'I have to, because if I don't, I cannot keep you safe, you or the baby. I couldn't keep *her* safe."

'Who?'

'Amelia.'

'Who is Amelia?'

'My sister.' He nodded, and she knew he was remembering everything he'd said the night they'd met.

'So badly did I want to paint,' he continued, 'so badly did I need an outlet for my pain that I left her. I left her at home. I locked her in her room to keep her safe, and then I snuck out. I thought she would be safe if I locked the door. If I kept them out.'

'Who out?' she asked, but he didn't hear.

'I thought… I promised myself I would only be out for an hour, and I was. But when I returned…she was gone. The fire has taken everything. I could have stopped it. I could have protected her if I'd have been there. If I hadn't been so selfish.'

'Your sister died in a fire?'

'She did,' he confirmed, and Aurora's heart broke for him.

Losing her parents had been hard. She had grieved. But losing Michael had been a different kind of a grief. A deeper pain.

'Sebastian…'

He dropped his hands to his sides and looked at her. The mist was gone, but the shadows lurked in his eyes.

'My hands do what I tell them to now,' he said. 'I create to please others now. I create for the people who need to see the light beyond their own darkness. I do not make art for me anymore. It is for them. For her.'

'For Amelia?' she asked.

'Yes!' he hissed. 'However unnatural it feels, I will keep my hands under control. Under my control.'

'You're punishing yourself?'

'I deserve it,' he said. 'My whole family is dead because I failed to protect them. And I failed you, too. I pushed you away in New York. I left you all alone and pregnant.'

'You didn't fail me,' she said. 'You are a gift.'

'I am no one's *gift*,' he snarled. 'But I will not fail again. I will not fail you. I will not make the same mistake.' He stepped back, away from her. 'I will keep my distance from you. I will keep my hands away. I will keep my head. Danger will never find you or our child.'

'Why would danger find us?' She stepped forward. Followed him. 'We're safe. You have made us safe. There's no one here but us. No one wants to hurt us…' Her body trembled, and her hand shook, but she made herself lift it. She pressed it to his chest, to the solid, unmoving muscle. 'I am here. Safe.' He inhaled deeply, and she felt it beneath his skin. He trembled too.

Aurora reached for his hand, and he let her claim it. Let her place it on the evidence of what they had made together.

Something beautiful.

Life.

'The baby is safe,' she assured him. 'There is no danger here. It is only us. Only what we could be. A family. A mother and father who are here for their child and each other. Friends. *More.*'

'Do you think because I live in a house, with a bed, I am civilised?' Sebastian murmured. 'You believe I'm safe? I was raised on the streets since I was fifteen. I'm not civilised. *I* am not safe.'

'Is that when it happened?' she asked. 'The fire?'

'It doesn't matter when it happened, it happened. I am still that man. That boy born into depravity, raised on the streets. You do not know me, Aurora. You do not know what I'm capable of. You do not want me to be your friend. Or lover. I am not capable of being either.'

'I think you are,' she countered, and her voice shook. 'I know you're a man of duty. A man who pretends not to care, but you care, deeply. You cared enough in the garden the night we met to help me through my grief. You are the man who cared about his unborn child enough to kidnap me. A man who donates the vast proceeds from his art to charity. You care whether or not you like it.'

'You are wrong.'

'I'm not,' she said. 'I've never been more right. So why not embrace it, Sebastian? Embrace this change? Embrace us?'

'Please go, Aurora,' he begged, but his hand remained on her stomach. All five tense digits curved around their baby.

He needed more time to accept this change that was happening between them.

'Okay.' She stood tall on the balls of her feet and leaned past the bump between them. 'One kiss and I'll go. If you still want me to.'

And she knew her words were an echo of that night. They both remembered how one kiss had not been enough.

He said nothing, but he didn't stop her as she leaned in. As she braced herself on his shoulders. And this time, she didn't aim for his cheek. She aimed for his mouth. For the kiss she needed to take. To give. To him.

She closed her eyes, and she kissed him with everything she had. She let him know she was here. With him.

She broke the seal of their mouths. Opened her eyes and met his.

'Listen to them,' she husked. 'Your hands, your body. Trust them and touch me the way you want to touch me. Kiss me the way you want to kiss me.'

He closed his eyes. His face contorted into a thousand lines of resistance. And she wanted to reach for each one, smooth them with her fingers. Her kisses.

'I do not know how,' he rasped, and pressed his forehead against hers. 'I do not trust myself to take only enough. I do not trust myself not to hurt you.'

'I trust you. All of you,' she told him. And she did. In ways she'd trusted no one.

Not only with her body, or her desires, but with her vulnerabilities, with the truth. However scared it made her feel, he'd allowed her to speak her truth from the moment they'd met. He'd allowed her to be honest with him about her wants, her needs.

She needed him now

And he needed her.

'Trust yourself, Sebastian,' she breathed. 'And—'

When she paused, he raised his head and stared into her eyes.

'Kiss me,' she demanded. 'Kiss me now.'

'It will be more than one kiss,' he admitted, voice raw.

'I know.'

'It will be...*more*.'

'I *want* more.'

He released a roar of both victory and defeat, and pressed his lips to hers.

And Aurora opened for him, took his pain and swallowed it whole. And she recognised the taste. It was an echo of her scream given back to her. The scream that had come from her when she'd thought she was all alone in the gardens the night they'd met. But she hadn't been alone. Just as he was not alone now. And she heard him, not only with her ears, not only with her body.

But with her heart.

CHAPTER NINE

Aurora's heart raged.

'Sebastian,' she breathed into his mouth, against the lips that were kissing her how she'd wanted to be kissed for weeks, months. Without hesitation. Without resistance.

His hands cradled her face, angled it softly, gently, as his tongue swept into her mouth. And she mewed for him as he tasted her. She pushed her tongue against his.

'*Oh*,' she moaned as he possessed her mouth. Claimed it as his. And it was his. It had only ever known his tongue. His taste. It was what she craved. What she'd yearned for since that night.

Him. *Only him.*

His hands moved. He swept the hair from her face, trailed his fingertips down the column of her throat, over her bare shoulders, down her arms, and she tingled. *Everywhere.*

His hands went to her waist. His lips pulled away from hers. But she knew this time he would come back to her without prompt or persuasion.

He was hers. As she was his.

This, them, it was fated.

Destiny.

'It will not be like last time,' he promised, and swept her into his arms. She knew she was safe with him.

He moved back towards the window. To the sun now throwing gentle rays onto the dark floor.

'I know,' she said, and touched his cheek. Stroked it.

His step faltered. He looked down into her upturned face. His cheeks were flushed. His pink lips parted enough for her to feel the shallow exhale of his breath touch her skin.

'I want to look,' he said. 'I want to see all of you.'

'Then look.'

He nodded. A single dip.

Gently he placed her on her feet before the window. Positioned her directly in the sun's warmth. And turned his back on her.

She didn't speak. She watched him. He moved to the sink with stealth and yanked free a felt tapestry from the wall beside it. But he didn't come back to her. He moved to the other wall and tore free the brown fur hanging there.

His eyes were black as he came towards her.

Her stomach somersaulted. A deep ache settled between her thighs. She reached for the tops of the spaghetti straps of her dress and pushed them off her shoulders.

'*No*,' he gritted out. 'Not yet.'

Her hands fell to her sides. Her heart raced harder, faster, as he knelt at her feet and spread out the tapestry. She now realised it was a pelt of soft, short fur.

'Here,' he said, and turned to her, held out his hand. 'Sit with me.'

She allowed his hand, warm and big, to close around hers, as he helped her down onto the floor with him.

They sat in front of each other on the makeshift bed.

The sunlight danced in his hair, which framed his face and fell to his shoulders. Her breath caught as she took in every line of his sculpted face.

'You're beautiful,' she husked, because it was true.

'No.' His hair moved forward as he shook his head. And she touched it. His chestnut hair was highlighted with grey and red. And it was like silk in her fingers. Feather-soft.

'Yes,' she corrected him. 'You are.'

His hand reached for her, and he stroked her own hair in return.

'The night I saw you in the gardens,' he said, 'I thought you weren't real, but a vision sent to torture me.'

'Torture you?'

'With your beauty,' he rasped. 'You lured me out because I wanted to see you, get closer to you. A siren calling me to my doom. My reckoning. I came willingly. And still you torture me. Because I want to see more. I want to touch all of you.'

'Then end it. This torture.' She sucked in a trembling breath. 'And touch me.'

'It will never end. I know this now.' He raised himself up on his knees until she looked up at him, and he down at her. 'I will only ever want more. More of your presence. Of your touch.' He pressed her down until her head met the pillow he'd made using the long furs. 'As I have every day, *every moment*, since we met.' And he leaned down, caught her lips and kissed her.

'*More*,' she demanded. 'I want more.'

His mouth moved, whispering kisses across the tip of her chin, her cheeks, the lids of her eyes.

He sat up on his knees, gazed down at her and tore the T-shirt from over his head. And she looked at him. At the broad shoulders, taut with strength. Power pulsed in his heaving, muscular chest. Her throat turned dry. Her mouth opened, her tongue seeking his tight pink nipples. Her eyes roved down to the prominent V leading down from his hips, lightly scattered with dark hair, and disappearing into his jeans.

'I will give you more.' He undid the button of his jeans, slid down the zip, and pushed them off with his boxers. Until he was naked at her feet. Proud and pulsing. '*Slowly*,' he promised thickly.

With unhurried hands, he undressed her. Pulled the lightweight stretchy dress down and over the bump protruding between them. Down over her thighs.

He gripped her ankles, one after the other, and pulled the dress free from her body until all she had on was her white knickers.

'I want to see all of you,' he growled, and reached for the white material sitting low on her hips. And slowly, agonizingly slowly, he took them down. His knuckles grazed the skin on her outer thighs.

'*Oh*,' she moaned, electrified.

He didn't pause. Didn't falter. He kept pulling the cotton down against her knees, down the tender flesh of her calves to her feet.

'Bend your knees,' he commanded, and she did just that. She bent her knees and planted her feet. Presented herself to him.

'Aurora,' he growled, his eyes moving over every naked inch of her skin. Her breasts, her darkened aureoles, her tight nipples. And down. Across her wide hips, her round stomach. His eyes rested on the dark triangle of curls between her legs. And she slickened. Felt the moisture coat her intimate lips.

'You are beauty itself,' he told her.

And she felt it. She felt precious. An artwork created just for his eyes. For his body. His hands.

Only for him.

He positioned himself between her knees. And ducked. Pressed his lips to the bone in her ankle and licked her.

'Sebastian!'

He didn't answer. He moved. Kissing upwards. Up her calf, her knee. Her inner thigh.

And then he kissed her there. At her core.

She squealed. Tried to lock her hips.

'I want to taste you.' He gripped her hips, pulled her onto his mouth and laved her with his tongue.

'Yes,' she panted, closing her eyes to encourage the intensity, or to diminish it, she didn't know. But the pleasure was overwhelming. Having his mouth on her. Kissing. Licking.

'Ahh!' She reached down and thrust her fingers into his hair as he caught the swollen nub at the centre of her and brought it between his lips. But he didn't relent as she pushed her head harder against her. He flicked his tongue and sucked until all she became was heat and trembling desire.

She didn't feel his hand leave her hip, but she knew it had when his finger pushed inside her. She clenched intimately around him. Rocked herself on the welcome digit. He pushed another inside her as his mouth worked her flesh.

And she was frantic. She clawed at him, tugging hair. Until all she could do was hold her breath and let it take over her. The warmth. So hot, so intoxicating was the illicit heat he dragged from inside her. It drugged her.

And she was helpless as the light burst in her abdomen. Behind her eyes.

She locked her thighs around his head.

And Aurora screamed.

Pressure unravelled in her every muscle. Loosened her, until her legs fell, her fingers unclenched. And she was breathless. Panting. She felt—

'Wonderful!' She opened her eyes, and they found him high above her. Watching her, with his eyes on fire. 'You are a gift!' she said, a light, breathless chuckle leaving her lips.

'Again?' he rasped, and she heard the question. Recognised it.

'Again,' she said, and gave him the permission to take what he needed. What they both desired.

More.

She lifted her legs to his waist and wrapped them as best she could around him.

'I want you,' she husked her truth. 'I need you inside me. Now.'

His eyes darkened.

He positioned the silken length of him at her core.

'I want you again, and again, until you have nothing left to give,' she told him. 'And I will take it all from you.'

'I will hurt you.'

'I can take it,' she said. 'I want it. All of you. And I will give you the same. All of me,' she promised, and waited. Watched him fight the fight he'd been battling since the gardens. Since the first time he'd let her kiss him and he'd kissed her in return.

But it was a fight he couldn't win.

There was only surrender.

Their surrender.

To each other.

'Aurora,' he growled, and he pushed inside her to the hilt. She was so full. Complete.

And she surrendered to it. Surrendered everything she was, and all she would become, to him.

And she felt him do the same. Surrender all he was. All he would become.

To her.

Her tightness wrapped around Sebastian in a silken fist.

He understood it now.

This pain.

This pleasure.

It was his punishment.

And he would bear it. Endure it. For her.

He gripped her hips and thrust.

'Sebastian!' She gasped his name, and he gritted his teeth. Watched her eyes widen. Watched the pleasure bleed into them. The pleasure he was giving her.

Endless pleasure.

It was a just punishment for his crime. For taking her into his arms, for using her, taking what he needed, and discarding her roughly with his seed inside her.

His eyes fell to the swell of her between them.

He'd left her vulnerable and alone.

He'd never leave her alone again.

She'd never be lonely.

'Deeper,' she urged. 'I need you deeper.'

Gently he took hold of her ankles resting on his hips and lifted them. 'If it is uncomfortable,' he said, and swallowed, attempting to wash the roughness from his voice, 'tell me.'

'What?' she panted.

He placed her legs on his shoulders. 'This.'

He moved his hips forward.

'Wow.' Her neck elongated, the muscles stretching long and taut. She squirmed into the makeshift pillow. 'Oh, wow.'

And his body strained. He hardened inside her until the agony had no end. He was so deep. Deeper than he'd ever wished to be inside another human being. And it was...*everything*. To be this deep inside her. To give her this. To give her what she wanted. When he had already taken so much from her.

He would take no more.

'*Please*,' she cried. 'Move.'

And he did. He moved inside her. Pulled himself out to the entrance of her core and thrust back in. He slid in and out of her, again and again, until his chest was on fire. His erection was so hard, so deep, it hurt.

And he accepted the pain.

'Oh, Sebastian!' Her breasts rose and fell rapidly. Heat deepened the red undertones of her skin.

She was a goddess, and he would worship her as such.

'Oh, please. *Oh, please!*'

She would never beg him again. Not for company. Not for his kiss. Not for pleasure. She deserved everything she'd asked for, and he'd give it to her. But he would always hold himself back. Restrain himself. Never hurt her with the force of his desire. He'd never take. Only give.

It was his compromise. It was the only way to keep her safe. To protect her and his child. To be with her. To use his arms and his body to hold her, to keep her close, but to never let her in. He would never get attached. He would never feel anything but *this*. A physical need he would sate in her body.

She clenched around him intimately.

He closed his eyes. It was so intense. Almost too much.

'Aurora!' He roared her name as she squeezed his pleasure from him and found her own.

And he was flying.

Pure euphoria made him feel weightless.

It was a pleasure he had never known, never knew could exist, and it lifted him higher and higher.

'Sebastian!'

He opened his eyes, and there she was beneath him as he soared above her, calling him back to her with open arms. To cushion his fall.

And he knew he'd let him himself fly too high. If he fell now, into her softness, into her arms, he would crush her with the force, the impact of him.

He would pull himself free, roll off her. Fall on his own.

'Again,' she said. 'I'm—'

'Aurora!' She arched her hips, took him deeper still. Massaged him tightly with the heart of her.

And he couldn't help it.

He fell.

Aurora caught him up in her arms.

And all he could do was breathe. Breathe her in. Her scent.

'That was amazing!' she sighed after minutes, hours. God only knew.

He raised himself on his elbows, prayed for the strength to return to him.

But he was weak.

How could this be a punishment when it felt so right? When *he* felt so right here in her arms?

It swept through him. Despite his bold words of punishment. Temptation teased at him. In his mind. Somewhere in his chest, it stroked. Her words, her promise of having what he never had. A family. That he didn't have to be alone.

But she did not know him.

She only knew this. The chemistry they shared. She didn't understand that he couldn't give her the type of family she wanted. Couldn't be the man she needed.

'Thank you,' she said, and smiled at him. Reached up and stroked his cheek.

And he knew he had only one response. He had more to say this time. More than a pitiful thank-you in return for what she had given him.

'We will try it your way,' he husked. 'We will be together as you want. In all the ways you suggested.'

'In what ways?'

'We will talk.' He leaned down and stopped a whisper from her lips. 'We will touch.'

She tilted her mouth. 'And kiss?' she added for him, and closed the distance between their lips until it was nothing but millimetres. Their heated breath mingled. And he yearned for the gap to close completely.

'Yes,' he breathed. 'We will kiss.'

Her lips feathered his. And he longed for more.

'We will do all the things a real couple do,' she said against his mouth.

'We will,' he said, and pushed his promise into her mouth with the tip of his tongue.

He'd give her everything she wanted. Everything but love. He had none to give. He did not deserve hers. But everything else.

This...

He deepened their kiss, and she moaned into his

mouth. His body pulsed, swelled, with the pleasure he was giving to her. The pleasure he'd continue to give until he couldn't.

Sebastian would embrace…change.

And he'd do it for her.

CHAPTER TEN

THUNDER BOOMED.

Aurora's sleep-heavy eyes flew wide open.

Yellow-white light crackled and lit up the sky outside. Water ran in a river down the panelled glass. The heavy drapes were open, and the next streak of lightning illuminated the room through the two large windows. Everything inside the room remained still, undisturbed by the storm.

The room dimmed as the lightning receded, but Aurora's restlessness remained. And it wasn't the wind or the thunder that disturbed her.

It was…

Slowly she turned her head on the once plump white pillow now indented from her head, from the pressure of her straining body after Sebastian had crept into bed that night. Slid beneath the heavy white linen, pressed his naked body against hers, and given her release. Again and again, until her listless body had clung to his, and she'd fallen into a deep, dreamless sleep.

She wasn't clinging to him now.

She wasn't asleep.

And it wasn't the storm that had woken her.

It was *him*.

'No...' he mumbled, his restless head arched, his thick neck straining. 'Please... *No!*'

'*Shush,*' she soothed, and reached between them, under the sheets, and placed her hand on his chest. It was solid. His muscles were so taut.

'Amelia...' Sweat beaded on his forehead. His chestnut hair streaked across his furrowed forehead was black from the moisture soaking his body.

She pushed it back, cleared his forehead with a gentle swipe of her palm. 'You're dreaming,' she said in a hushed whisper.

'I'm sorry...' Tremors raked through his body. 'I'm so sorry...' he croaked on a barely contained sob, and that broke something inside her.

When Michael had died, she'd had so many dreams. Dreams of all the things she should have done and hadn't. She'd woken tear-drenched and raked with guilt. All alone.

He wasn't alone now.

She couldn't see what was doing it. Hurting him. But she could stop whatever was invading his sleep. She could make it go away.

'Sebastian.' She sat up beside him, stroked his broad bare shoulders. 'Wake up.'

Lightning crackled.

His eyes opened, wide and haunted. He looked up at her but he didn't speak. His face haggard, he stared at her, his breathing deep and uneven.

Emotion bubbled in her chest. Her eyes crowded with tears.

'What was she like?'

'Who?' he rasped roughly.

She couldn't help it. A tear slipped free.

He cleared his throat. 'Why are you crying?' His hand lifted to her cheek. The pad of his big thumb caught the tear. Wiped it away.

'For you,' she said. 'And Amelia.'

His hand fell to his side. Focus returned to his glazed eyes with sharp intensity. 'What did I say?'

'You were dreaming,' she explained.

His brow furrowed. 'I haven't dreamt of her for over a decade.'

He threw a hand over his eyes. Hid the shadows that had entered his eyes with the sound of his sister's name.

And she wouldn't let him do it again. Hide from her.

For two weeks, they had been together. They'd shared every meal. They had touched. Kissed. Every night, he'd climbed into her bed beside her, learnt her body and she his with a famished, ravenous intensity.

But talk? They'd shared words, talked about the baby, shared pleasantries about their meals...but she had still not passed the surface level of Sebastian.

And she wanted in. She wanted in desperately.

'Don't,' she said, and reached for his hand, pulled it away from his eyes and drew it towards her. Held it.

His eyes shuttered. 'Don't what?'

'Don't hide from me.'

'I'm right here.' He dragged his free hand through his hair. 'Where I have been every day, every night, for two weeks? With you.'

He pulled his hand free from her grasp, shifted his hips backwards and sat up against the intricately designed wooden headboard spanning the width of the bed and reaching to the ceiling.

He turned to her, opened his arms wide. 'Come,' he said. 'Come here.'

Thunder rumbled. More quietly now. The storm was moving. But Aurora understood she had a choice. She could crawl between his legs, sit on his lap and let him stir her tired body to life.

Or she could invite the storm inside.

Ignoring the heat stirring in her pelvis, she made a choice.

'No,' she said.

He turned from her, flipped on the beside lamp. The room filled with a soft amber artificial light. But he didn't reach for her again. He dropped his hands into his lap covered by the white sheet, low on his lips.

He arched a brow. 'No?'

She inhaled deeply, straightened her spine, and said more firmly, 'No.'

'Why not?'

'Because you're hurting.'

'I am not in pain.'

'But you were,' she pointed out. 'And your body remembers it, even if you don't want to acknowledge it. You *still* hurt enough for it to infiltrate your dreams.'

'It's only a dream.' He dismissed her with a flippant wave of his hand.

'It's your mind, consciously or subconsciously,' she said tightly, 'and it's telling you—'

'It tells me nothing I don't already know.'

'But I don't know,' she reminded him. 'And I want to. I want to know what your sister was like?'

'What does it matter what she was like?' he snarled, baring perfectly white teeth. 'She's dead.'

'But you're not.' She swallowed. 'And your sister lives inside you. In your dreams…' She blew out a breath, wanting him to understand, to let him know she understood, even if she didn't know all the facts, but she didn't know how to do it. How to show him.

'Do you talk about her?' she asked. *'Ever?'*

'No.'

'I don't talk about Michael either. I thought it would hurt too much. It *did* hurt in the gardens when I told you a little of him, of our relationship, and what happened to him. But I didn't tell you everything, and I... I think it hurts more not tell it. To not talk about him. All of him. Not just his death.'

'You want to talk about him now?'

She nodded.

'Tell me,' he said. 'Tell me about Michael.'

'He was...' She sucked in a lungful of fortifying breath. 'He was my big brother, and I loved him. I looked up to him. I envied him in the earlier days.'

'Why would you envy him?'

'He was always so...*free*.'

'Free?'

'He never put on a show. He never pretended to be anything other than what he was. Cheeky, naughty. Innocent things when we were young. Speaking out of turn. Playing pranks.' She swallowed. 'Harmless things, really.'

'Did you play pranks, too?' he asked gently.

Her chest tightened. 'Once.'

'And what happened?'

'It was silly,' she said, remembering. 'I collected worms from the garden and put them in the new nanny's bed. I didn't like her. She was mean.'

'She hurt you?'

'Only with words. But our parents assumed it was Michael, and I let them believe it. I let him take the blame, and he did. Not once did he tell them it wasn't him. And

I started to lean into that. I wanted them to love me,' she confessed roughly. 'I pretended to be the golden child that day, and it became my role. I dedicated myself to it. To being perfect.'

'You are perfect.'

'I'm not,' she said. 'I wasn't. I leaned into Michael's misbehaviour to amplify my own goodness, because I wanted their approval, but they always withheld it anyway. Michael's behaviour grew worse...'

'How?' he pressed softly. 'How did it get worse?'

'It was light stuff at first,' she said. 'Parties. Smoking. Cannabis.' She swallowed, remembering finding him in the gazebo, reeking. 'He said it was a one-off. Then he promised he only did it when he needed to relax. When he had to come home to *them*. He was lying. He smoked it all the time. I could smell it. But I believed him. I believed it was harmless. That his habit wouldn't progress.'

'But it did?'

'He took harder stuff, until I couldn't see him behind his bleary red eyes.' Aurora scrunched up her nose to stem the burn there. 'My parents put so much pressure on us. On Michael, and he escaped it, them, with gambling highs and drugs. But the Michael I grew up with, who protected me from our parents' put-downs and took them all for himself, was gone, long before my parents abandoned him. Before I did. He was gone before he died. I realise that now.'

Pain lanced her through the chest. 'But the night my parents threw him out, he begged me to believe he could change, would change.' A tear fell, and she let it fall. 'I didn't believe him. I let him go off on his own because I didn't want to risk my parents' wrath, their displeasure. I wanted to be good. To be loved. To be the golden child.

And then Michael died. *Alone*, because I had been manipulated into being the daughter they wanted.' She hissed, disgusted at what she'd let herself become to please her parents. Who, she realised now, would never have been pleased with her. Not obedient Aurora. Not rebellious Aurora.

'Don't cry.'

'How can I not?' she said. 'I didn't believe him. I didn't give him a chance, not even one last chance to change, because I was too afraid to stand by his side and fail with him. And what did I achieve not lobbying for him one last time? Nothing. I became the heiress to the Arundel name and fortune because I was the only one left. And they thought I'd look after it when they were dead, how they wanted it to be looked after. But after you...after New York, I realised I didn't have to do it their way. I could live my life how I chose to.'

'And what choices did you make for your life?'

'I chose to continue being the person I became the night I met you,' she confessed. 'To be brave and bold in the choices I make now.'

She searched his eyes, and she saw nothing but shadows.

If he wouldn't let her in, she'd climb inside herself. Talk to the shadows he wouldn't recognise still took up too much space in his mind. *His dreams.*

She moved her body until she was on her knees. Her blue dotted nightgown rose to her thighs as she crawled onto his naked lap.

'Aurora...' He held up his hands in the air as she settled herself, her thighs on either side of his. The baby was big and round between them. 'What are you doing?'

'You need to talk about them, like I did,' she said.

'You need to talk about her. Amelia. You need to face your demons, and—'

'My demons are my own.'

'You can't control them.'

'I can.'

'No, not until you face them,' she said, realizing now it was the truth. 'Or they will own you. Mind, body and soul. Forever.'

She could almost touch it, see it, standing between them. A real-life demon blocking the connection between them that could be so much stronger if he allowed it to flow freely.

If only he talked to her.

Really talked.

'No. Aurora, I can't give you this. I have given you everything else, but I can't give you this.' His hands moved, and he stroked her hair. He coiled his fingers in it and tugged, not enough to hurt, but enough for her to feel the tension, the strength, in his hands. 'I will not put the images that haunt my dreams into your pretty little head. I won't dump my trauma into your innocent mind. I don't want you to know it.'

'But I want to know you, and whatever has happened is a part of you.'

'It's not a part you need.'

'So you'll keep it all to yourself?' she asked, undeterred. 'You'll continue to lock yourself away? I could have done that,' she almost shouted, but she didn't. 'I could have done what you did. Locked myself away in Arundel Manor with my grief and my guilt. But I didn't. I am here, with you, because *I* didn't.'

'We are not the same. You don't know—'

His jaw locked.

She searched his eyes. Those amber-and-green-filled depths. And she wanted to break down the walls surrounding him, but only he could do that.

'Then tell me,' she urged. 'Tell me everything.'

And she waited...

Hadn't she just revealed her own wound? Her own guilt? Hadn't they both tried to be something they weren't, something they shouldn't have had to be, for other people?

Their stories were so similar and yet so different.

His throat squeezed tightly.

She made it sound so easy to make a different choice. There were no different choices for him. But she was here, so soft, so determined to...help him.

No one had ever wanted to help him. Esther... He was money for her, pure and simple. Over time, she'd grown loyal. Loved him. *Maybe*. But Aurora... She had no reason to demand this of him, other than that she naively thought this would change something in him.

It wouldn't change anything. So why not tell her?

It might make her leave.

His stomach tensed. If he didn't tell her, she might leave too. Either way, it was a chance. A risk he wouldn't take.

It was only a story...

'There is no official story of my life before...' He was unsure where to begin.

'Tell me the unofficial one.'

'I have told no one about it,' he said. 'No one knows about the before.'

'No one?'

He shook his head. 'As far as the world knows, I'm

Sebastian Shard, born the moment my agent Esther discovered me on the streets. Already a man.'

'But that isn't true.'

'No,' he said honestly. 'I was young, once. But I never really had a childhood, was never allowed one. I was never allowed to play with any other children. I was locked in a basement.'

He felt Aurora's gaze narrow. 'A basement?'

He nodded stiffly. 'I decorated it. I drew, I painted, on any surface I could from the moment I knew how. I turned it into our secret place,' he said, remembering the mural of a never-ending horizon of deep reds and burnt oranges. He swallowed thickly. 'Mine and Amelia's. Until the basement was gone, until we moved into a house with a man. A man who told me to call him Daddy.'

'Your stepfather?'

'He was never a father to me.' His necked corded. 'He was barely a man.' His hands clenched on the bedspread. 'He was my mother's pimp,' he spat.

'Your mother was a prostitute?'

'Yes,' he admitted, and it hurt to tell her. For her to know the shame he felt. 'We always lived in a shared house before... There were women everywhere. *I* knew what it was when I was seven, maybe eight. Maybe younger... Those women weren't my aunts. It wasn't a shared house. It was a brothel. Run by my mother.'

Her eyes flew wide open. 'She was a *madam*?'

'Yes.'

'Surely someone knew? A teacher? A doctor? Someone who could have taken you out of there? Put you into foster care? A family home?'

'It *was* a family, of sorts.' His blood heated. 'Before him.'

'Someone had to know there were children inside of a brothel!'

'There is no record of me. My home birth was undocumented, as was Amelia's. There was no one to know. We didn't exist officially.'

'But a midwife?' she asked. 'Surely a midwife was there to help your mum give birth?'

'When I was a child, there were always women around in various stages of dress,' he explained. 'There was enough of a collective of experience that there was no need for outside help.'

'How is that possible?' She frowned. 'This isn't the dark ages. Children aren't… Their existence isn't…unknown.'

'Children are missing to the system all the time, Aurora. And their existence is obsolete because it isn't on some computer,' he said too harshly.

He couldn't help it. He was angry at her for pushing him, angry at himself for telling. But it pulsed through him. A small part of him itched to tell the story he never had told anyone. To her. To have her understand him.

'It's not a pretty story. I don't know how to tell it without the ugly bits. I don't want the ugly bits in your head… I don't want to talk about it while you are on my lap.' His hands moved of their own volition. Touched her soft upper arms, and he stroked them. Soothed the ache in his fingers against her silky skin. 'You are so soft,' he said. 'So innocent.'

'Then tell me the pretty bits first.'

'There were no pretty things about my life,' he said. 'Until you.'

She smiled, but it didn't reach her eyes. 'Tell me about Amelia.'

'She died,' he said thickly. 'When she was three.'

'What about the three years she lived?'

'She...' Emotion clogged his throat.

Fingers, feather-light, stroked his cheek. 'It's okay to remember her.'

Was it? Was it okay to think of her tiny fingers? Fingers that had clung to him, trusted him. He had left her alone to die.

He closed his eyes. Shut out the trusting eyes clinging to his. He would not fail the trust Aurora placed in him. *Never*.

Lips, so smooth and soft, kissed his cheek. 'It's going to hurt,' she breathed against his skin as her lips moved to the tip of his nose and over to his other cheek.

'It will hurt to remember her happy,' she continued, and Aurora kissed him again. 'It'll hurt to know that, however happy she was, she died. But you have to remember more than her death, Sebastian.'

She kissed his eyelids now. His right one, then his left. And Sebastian trembled.

'You have to remember.' Her lips feathered his forehead. 'Remember how she lived. How she was part of your life. How she still is. Face whatever guilt it is you feel, and let yourself move on. Forgive yourself.'

His eyes flew open. He caught the wrists moving from his chest to hold his face. He wouldn't let her cradle his cheeks and push her innocence inside his skin with her gentle fingers.

He was not innocent.

He released her wrists and caught her waist.

'Sebastian!'

He ignored her. He could not have her on his lap. He could not feel her warmth when his blood ran so cold.

He lifted her, made his hands be careful, and placed her on the bed beside him.

'Sebastian,' she said. *'Please.'*

And it hurt him for her to beg. For him to break his promise to never to let her beg for anything from him. But this time, she was wrong. *This*…he could not change. He couldn't undo what he'd done.

'I will never forgive myself,' he hissed. His chest was so tight. 'She was beautiful. Innocence personified. She was the definition of it, with her curly black hair, her little button nose that squinched with her squinting big blue eyes when she laughed. And she laughed all the time. In our room we shared. A room with everything we needed, a kitchen. A bathroom. And I fed her. I burped her. *I loved her!*'

'I know,' she breathed heavily.

'You do not know. You do not know what it is like to have something precious given to you. Something so innocent you cannot help but love it.'

'I'm pregnant,' she said. 'Soon we'll both be given something precious. Something we will both love.' She placed her hand on her belly. 'I feel the baby all the time. Its tiny hands. Its feet. *I* understand that kind of love. The consuming nature of it. I understand how much you loved her.'

He dragged his hands through his too long hair. Pushed it back away from the skin that crawled with self-hate. *Self-disgust.*

He closed his eyes. Shut out Aurora. Her misted big brown eyes. He didn't deserve her compassion. And he'd tell her why. And then he'd open his eyes. Watch her tears disappear. Watch the shame he felt reflected in her eyes with the ugly images he'd now put into her beautiful, determined, naive, and stubborn mind.

He was not naive.

'Love is never enough,' he hissed, his eyes still closed. 'I was given a responsibility. To take care of her. And I did. I held her. I provided for her every need from the moment she was born. Because in the rooms beyond ours... the other rooms, filled with women. With men. Drinking. Having sex. Doing drugs. It wasn't safe for her there. But we were safe in our room. She was safe with *me*.'

'How old were you?'

He squeezed the bridge of his nose. 'I was twelve, and she was brand new. And she'd relied on me. And for three years, I kept her safe. I protected her. Until one night, while she was asleep in her crib beside my bed, I—'

He would tell her. However hard it was to admit. To thrust the words into her ears and have her know.

She had a right to know who she had made love to in New York.

She had a right to know who the man was she shared her bed with now.

He opened his eyes, and he hid nothing from her. He let her look into his eyes and see the man he was.

Unworthy.

'The house was full. All the rooms were occupied, and the others who didn't have rooms spilt into the lounge, the kitchen,' he told her, and he let the images bloom to life in his head. The open sex. *The depravity.*

'Our room was at the top of the house this time,' he continued. 'It was a beautiful house. In a neighbourhood where no one would ever expect such ugliness to live. Unlittered and privileged, the neighbourhood was picturesque. All of it was. All but our house. But our room had a lock. And I wanted to get out. I wanted to breathe the night's air... Needed to paint, to draw, do something with my hands.'

He looked down at them. The hands trembling before him. 'To create the images I never found in life. Images of softness, of hope. And so I left her. I left Amelia sleeping in our room. I locked the door so no one would hurt her. I locked the door to keep her safe. I left, and I took the key...'

'Sebastian...' She cried openly now. Big, rolling tears dripped from the tip of her beautiful chin.

He had to stop her tears.

In the end, she would not pity him.

'I stayed out for an hour, no more...'

'The fire,' she said, and faster her tears fell.

His blood turned to ice. It ran into his bones. Threatened to shatter them to nothing but dust.

'When I came back... The house was gone. It was nothing but smoke and ash. Some survived. They stood with firemen or sat inside ambulances. But Amelia was gone. The top of the house... It was still smoking. She was...*dead*.'

Aurora swiped at her cheeks with the backs of her hands. And then she looked at him, her chest moving up and down as rapidly as his own. She lifted her arms and held them wide. 'Come to me,' she said.

'I will not.'

'Come to me,' she demanded again, and his body ached with his resistance to fall into her arms.

'I do not want your pity,' he growled. 'I do not deserve it.'

'You deserve everything,' she corrected him.

'Have you heard *nothing*?'

'I heard every word,' she said, still holding those dainty arms open for him.

'You were a child taking care of his sister in a house that should never have existed with children inside it. But you existed. Both of you did. And you made that existence bearable for your sister because you loved her. And you wanted a moment for yourself, and you did what you thought was right. You tried to keep her safe.'

'And I failed.'

'Your mother failed you. From the moment you were born, from the moment she thrust Amelia into your arms. It wasn't your fault. Forgive yourself, Sebastian.'

'Never.'

She rose on her knees. 'I'm going to hold you.'

'I do not want you to.'

'But I'm going to,' she said. 'I'm going to hold the little boy who needed someone to hold him. I'm going to hold you, the man who needs to be held because he has been alone for far too long. He has locked himself away for years because he blamed himself for something that was never his fault—' Her voice broke.

Something tore inside him. In his chest.

'It *was* my fault.'

'It wasn't,' she said, and she sat in front of him on her knees. 'But you've punished yourself enough.'

'It will never be enough.'

She brushed the tears away, but her eyes pleaded. 'Let me hold you.'

'I do not want your arms around me,' he lied, because all his body craved was her.

'Turn the light off.'

His gaze narrowed. 'Why?'

She gripped the hem of her nighty, tore it over her head and threw it on the ground.

'What are you doing?' he growled.

'I'm getting into bed.'

And she did.

He looked at her lying beside him.

'Hold me,' she said. But she kept her head where it was. Her head on the pillow. Her eyes pointing at the wall. 'I need you to hold *us*.'

His body roared.

How could he deny her? He'd promised to meet all her needs. Physically at least.

He couldn't help it. His body wouldn't listen to his demand to stay still. To keep his hands away from her.

He flipped the light off. Slipped his hips down the bed and turned. Moulded his body to the shape of her.

She grabbed his wrists, his hands, and wrapped them around her. Around *them*.

He closed his eyes. 'Aurora—'

'Don't talk. You don't have to say anything else,' she told him. 'Just hold me and know I'm right here with you. *We* are.'

Tears filled his eyes.

He wouldn't shed them.

'Tomorrow, we'll find a way to honour the boy you were. The children like you,' she whispered. 'Tomorrow, we'll find a way to honour Amelia.'

'There is no honour to be found.'

'Sleep, Sebastian.'

And with his heart hammering, Sebastian closed his eyes. Let his mind only hear her. Her breathing. He did not examine the intimacy of the moment she was giving to him. But he knew it was the most intimate moment he'd ever had.

In this moment, he was closer to her than he'd ever been to anyone.

She understood he would not let her soothe him, and so she had asked him to soothe her. And she knew he wouldn't refuse her request, because...

She knew *him*.

She knew what he was, what he'd done, and still she wanted him here.

The knowledge shattered him. He felt raw. Broken open, and all that kept him together was her. Her body pressed against his. The rhythmic lull of her soft exchange of air calmed something inside him. Her soft, small hands on top of his. She was holding their baby *with* him.

It was everything he shouldn't have.

Everything he didn't deserve.

But here it was.

Here they were.

His family.

And he held them both in his big, greedy hands. Because he was a glutton. *Selfish.*

But he couldn't let go of her.

He would never let them go.

A fatigue, so heavy, blanketed his mind.

He was so tired...

Darkness claimed him. And Sebastian slept a dreamless sleep, holding on to Aurora.

And she held him right back.

CHAPTER ELEVEN

THE KITCHENS HUMMED with activity and a thousand scents.

Aurora walked, one red silk pump after the other, through the white shirts and black waistcoats of the staff working diligently away in the smaller kitchen preparing the silver serving trays. The champagne glasses sparkled as the bubbles rose to the top. The canapés were the perfect size for the guests who were beginning to enter the great dining hall.

'Mind your backs,' a chef called as she stepped into the bigger second kitchen.

She stopped at the roasting trays, pulled from the ovens by the team of chefs in their whites. The trays steamed. The smell of tiny quails, smothered in herbs and butter, assaulted her airways, but she resisted the urge to stick her fingers in the juices and lick them.

She'd eat them soon enough at the head table with Sebastian.

'Miss Arundel?' She turned her back to the chefs, ignored the grumble of her stomach, and focused on the bright blue eyes of the event coordinator, Tina.

She was a godsend. Without her and Esther, she couldn't have pulled it off in a week. But together they had pulled it off in an afternoon.

Her stomach twinged. She was right to rush this—to rush him. Their time was almost up. The baby would be here in three weeks...

'What's wrong?' Aurora asked when those blue eyes, wide with worry, stared at her unblinkingly.

Tina pushed the microphone of her headset away from her lips. 'Nothing.' She smiled. A perfect smile. But Aurora wasn't fooled. It was brittle.

'Something's wrong,' Aurora said. 'The hall isn't ready, is it?'

She shook her head. 'The dining hall's ready,' she said. 'The guests are arriving and are being shown in.' She waved to the staff exiting the outer kitchen. 'The staff are taking the canapés out now...'

'So, then, what is it?'

'Esther Mahoti is here.'

'Is she?'

Aurora couldn't wait to meet her in person. A no-nonsense woman who had supplied everything Aurora needed to make today a success. She'd curated the perfect guest list, deployed the teams of staff to ready the castle. She'd planned, with her team, the transport for the guests, organised the art team to install Sebastian's pieces in the dining hall, and personally sent Aurora the silk pumps on her feet.

'She is.' Tina swallowed. 'And she's demanding to see Mr Shard.'

'Then show her to him.'

'I can't find him.' Panic tightened the slender throat inside the baby-pink necktie. 'I'm supposed to know where he is. Where *everyone* is. And Esther—'

'Will be fine,' she soothed, but her throat was tightening too.

'She'll never use our event company again if I lose the star of the show.'

'Bring Esther into the hall. Let her see what you've accomplished in such short notice.'

'It won't be enough. If I can't deliver Mr—'

'I'll deliver him.' Aurora tucked Tina's arm in hers and walked her back out the way she'd come.

Her stomach flipped. Was he ready? Had she demanded too much? Too quickly. Too fast.

'Do what you do best.' She smiled tightly. 'We'll be with you soon,' she promised.

Tina flipped her headset back into place and walked off, talking into it in hushed whispers.

Aurora watched her leave, turned on her heel, and pushed through the side door to the back of the courtyard.

Her heart raced. This morning Sebastian had kissed her forehead and told her he was going for a walk. Alone. It wasn't unusual. Since the night he'd told her about Amelia, he'd claimed more and more moments for himself. But he'd always returned to her by nightfall and climbed into bed beside her.

Aurora moved out of the side gate. She looked up at the skies. A helicopter whirred. It descended the mountains lined with trees. More guests.

She dropped her gaze to the trees standing guard at the entrance of the forest. She moved towards them, over the field of short green grass.

She'd find him.

Aurora stepped into the forest. Twigs broke underfoot as she took herself deeper into the overlapping trees.

'Sebastian?' she called, but all that answered her were the birds she'd startled, flying upwards to higher branches.

White beams of light shone through the branches overhead, scattered with drooping leaves.

She closed her eyes and listened.

She could hear running water.

She opened her eyes, listening, finding the right direction...

She moved toward the sound of rippling water, and it got closer with her every step.

Her feet halted at the top of an incline. A slow-flowing river moved below. A natural stairway of roots led the way down through the trees. She took them, step after step, down to the river. As she did, the trees parted.

And the view stole her breath.

'*There* you are. I found you,' she husked, stopping still.

He stood from where he knelt next to the river. And she watched him rise. Watched the sun play with the wisps of his hair hanging loose at his shoulders. His open-collared white shirt revealed the thick hair-covered throat. And up her eyes went. To the tip of his bristled chin, to linger on his plump pink lower lip. Up the length of his noble nose. To his eyes. Green-and-amber depths staring straight at her.

'I wasn't lost,' he said deeply.

She moved towards him. Her heart racing. Her body tightening, urging her closer. *Nearer.*

He had been lost. They both had in New York.

Would he tell her the same now as he had then? That he wasn't hers to find.

She cleared her throat. 'What are you doing down here?'

'Thinking.'

'And what have you been thinking about all morning?' she asked, her lips moving into a smile. But her lips were too heavy, her lungs too breathless to perform the ease she wanted to portray.

She wasn't at ease. The air hummed with it. A restlessness. And it made the hairs rise beneath her red-silk-covered arms.

'You,' he said, and his eyes dropped to her stomach. Rounded and obvious beneath the folds of her red sparkly gown. 'And the baby.'

She stopped before him. The moss-covered ground was soft beneath her shoes. 'What about us?'

'They have breached the walls,' he said. 'The doors are wide open. And in they go. Into my house.' His eyes rose to meet hers. 'You invited them inside.'

His eyes were not accusing. His voice was soft, and yet she felt like a traitor.

'We talked about this.' She exhaled heavily. They had talked about it the morning after he'd told her about Amelia. Lay in bed together. Naked. Holding each other. 'We decided to do it together for Amelia,' she reminded him. 'And we are doing it. *Today.*'

'I'm no speechmaker, Aurora,' he said. 'I don't stand in great halls, or on podiums, in front of people like them and talk. I do not talk about myself.'

'This isn't about you,' she said, knowing it was a half truth. It was the only part he would hear. The only reason he would do this was for her. But she understood he needed it far more than Amelia did now.

'They don't care,' he scoffed. 'They want what my hands create. They want my work. They don't care what Amelia endured. People like them, privileged and elite, ignore what happens in houses like the one I grew up in, houses next door to their own. They pretend that what happens inside those houses doesn't happen. But they know, Aurora. How could they not?' he said, his top lip lifting to expose gritted white teeth. 'They fear what lives in the dark, so they choose to be ignorant. To ignore it. They ignored Amelia's suffering.'

She wanted to touch him. Reach out and hold his hand. But he had to trust her enough to take it.

'I wish I'd stood on a podium,' she said. 'I wish I'd made my parents listen one last time. Made them realise Michael needed help. He needed love. Unconditional love...'

Her heart raced.

Love. There it was in her mind. On her tongue. And it didn't feel wrong to think it. To feel it.

She was in love with him.

She pushed it down. Today wasn't about her.

'I wish,' she breathed, 'I had used my voice before now. I wish I'd realised sooner the shame they made me feel about Michael, his condition, his addictions... It was nothing to be shameful about. It was an opportunity to expose the awful atrocities not only the rich experience, but the less fortunate.'

'They don't care, Aurora.'

'Then make them care.' She puffed out air. 'Stand in front of them as Sebastian Shard and tell them the causes they are donating to are worthy. The people that experience these awful things are worthy.'

That you *are worthy*, she added silently, because he wouldn't want to hear it. Nor would he accept it.

He had to believe today was for Amelia.

His lips firmed into a flat line. 'How am I supposed to do that?' he asked.

'Without shame,' she said, swallowing all the emotion in her chest that was threatening to clog her throat.

'You, Amelia...the children who have experienced, are still experiencing, the same things that you did...they have nothing to be embarrassed about. It isn't their fault the world is ugly sometimes, that it exposes them to unspeakable things.'

'But it was my fault that she died,' he corrected her. 'Am I supposed to tell them that? That I locked her in?'

'Yes,' she said. 'If you want to tell them your and Amelia's story, tell them. You did nothing wrong.'

'And what?' he snarled. Baring his perfectly white teeth. 'Stand up there and shame you. Tell the world that the baby inside you was put there by a man who abandoned his family. Left them to—'

'You abandoned no one,' she interjected sharply. 'You haven't abandoned us.'

His cheek pulsed. 'I want them to know you will be my wife.'

'Sebastian...' Her heart danced. She wanted to be that. To be his wife. She wanted to be his.

But not like this.

He thrust his hand into his pocket. He withdrew his hand, clenched in a fist, and held it out between them.

'Marry me.' He opened his hand, and there in his palm sat a ring of twisted silver, at its centre the bluest stone she'd ever seen.

'It is the same colour as your dress the night we met,' he said. 'Siren's blue.'

Her hand lifted. She couldn't stop it. She touched this ring that would bind her to him.

In name.

Her heart smashed against her ribs. She wanted more than twisted silver.

She dropped her hand, raised her eyes to his.

She wanted…

Her eyes filled with unwanted tears.

She wanted his heart. To *be* his heart. To be loved as intensely as he loved his art. As he had loved Amelia.

'Wear it, Aurora,' he urged. 'Our baby will not be undocumented. It will never be lost in the dark. Let them know I am your protector. Let them know Sebastian Shard, the enigma that creeps around in the dark and creates images that haunts them, protects you and our child.'

She wanted more. More than protection.

She wanted everything.

Everything he wasn't ready to give.

She reached for his fingers and closed them around the ring. 'Let's not talk of marriage today,' she said. 'But… I'll stand there beside you, whatever you choose to say, and I'll be proud to have them know you're the father of my child. You don't have to hide in the dark anymore, Sebastian.'

'Aurora…' His Adam's apple danced. 'They fear the dark. They fear the noises that come out of the shadows,' he told her fiercely. 'I am the dark, and they will fear me.'

'No.' She dropped her hands to her sides. 'You and Amelia were made to stay in the shadows. To hide. Don't make Amelia hide anymore.'

'She is dead, Aurora,' he said without venom, only acceptance. 'I understand what you have tried to do today, but opening the doors makes me weak.'

'You are not weak,' she corrected him quietly. 'You and Amelia deserve to exist. To be seen. Stand in front of them, Sebastian,' she urged, 'and tell them what you think is right.' She knew she was pushing him hard, but… 'Stand in front of them and tell them Amelia's story. Make them know *her* story. Make them see her. Make her death mean something. Something that can change things for other undocumented—*invisible*—children.'

His nostrils flared.

'You have an opportunity to not only donate your art to causes you believe in, but to be the face of it. Your face, without a mask, without hiding behind the art you make.' She swallowed. 'Today they are all here. So stand in front of them as yourself. For Amelia. Don't hide anymore, Sebastian. Make them see—'

'Me?'

'Yes,' she agreed, and she waited. Even though their time was almost up. The afternoon gala was ready to proceed...but he needed time, and she'd give him a little more.

He nodded and pocketed the ring. Then he did it. He pushed his fingers between hers. Entwined them until the pads of his fingers pressed against her knuckles.

'For Amelia,' he said, 'and after...' His throat bulged.

'After?'

'You will wear my ring,' he said, and pulled her into step beside him.

Aurora's heart swelled.

She knew the truth.

Today, it was for him.

She squeezed his hand tighter and let him lead her up the stairs of wood.

And after...

Her heart soared.

She'd marry him for herself. But only for the right reason.

For love.

Sebastian guided Aurora out of the forest. *Slowly.*

He swallowed the urge to lift her, to tell her off again

for taking stairs too steep and uneven, to find him. She wouldn't listen.

She'd delight in telling him that despite his vows, despite his decision not to care for her too deeply, to care about anything or anyone, he did. He cared.

And she was right. He did not want her to be. But he… cared. *Deeply.*

He'd shared himself with her, not only physically, but in ways he'd never shared himself before. He hadn't used pretty pictures he created to express himself. With her, he'd used words, given her ugly images that haunted him, voiced his thoughts, and confessed his crimes. He'd revealed to her the man he was beneath his name.

Yet still she held his hand.

And despite himself, he enjoyed, craved even, her ability to prove him wrong.

She'd shown him that he could change.

They stepped out of the forest, and the trees shook with the wind, pushing them forward. He stopped, bringing them to a halt on the edge of the tree line. He watched the air lift the black silk kissing her shoulders.

'You are stunning, Aurora,' he growled, his voice raw.

'Thank you' she responded. 'I feel beautiful.' The edges of her painted plum lips curved upwards, and he couldn't help it. So did his. He smiled. Until the muscles he hadn't used in such a long time ached.

'Very, *very* beautiful,' he agreed.

The wind swept through the trees again. *Harder.* Red, brown and orange leaves left their branches. They scattered and fell around them like confetti.

And he knew it. In this moment, he wasn't the only one to embrace change. She *had* changed. No longer was she the broken creature screaming into the trees. She was vibrant. Confident. And it was so easy to feed from her youth, from her unbreakable confidence that her way was the right way.

Clarity cleared the last remaining doubts from his mind. The fog lifted, and so did something inside him.

She was right, *had* been right, before she'd known his name, his face...

She had known him the moment their eyes had met.

She'd known their worlds colliding was the beginning.

The beginning of something special.

She *was* his awakening.

This goddess in red silk, sparkling with stardust, was his reckoning.

His redemption.

She cocked her head to the side. 'Ready?'

He nodded.

He was.

Because of her.

His Aurora...

They both stepped forward, toward the castle, and he realised neither led the other. They walked together. Side by side. Hand in hand, out of the shadows, and into the full beam of a too bright sun.

He was not alone.

And it did not feel like weakness to have her beside him.

It was power.

She was his power, and she fortified him. Strengthened him in this choice to claim this opportunity she'd given to him with her small hand holding his. An opportunity to stand as himself and bring Amelia with him out of the shadows. To give his name and his face to a charity he would found to support children like her. Forgotten children.

And he would do it. Today.

He would no longer let the rich and the privileged elite remain ignorant.

He would make them look.

He would make them see more than his pretty art.

And they would acknowledge what they feared.

They would acknowledge *him*. All that he was, and all that he had become despite them.

Together, he and Aurora crossed the courtyard and entered the castle. Together, they walked down the corridor lined with a thousand windows. Long, heavy black drapes hung from the walls, tied with gold twine that held them open, let the light in. And on they went until they came to the two tall doors made of oak and iron. But neither stopped as Sebastian dipped his head and the staff on either side of the doors opened them.

Sebastian and Aurora swept into the great hall.

Together.

Hand in hand, they strode down the white carpeted central aisle between the circular oak tables of white cloth and silver cutlery to the front of the room.

They took to the stage, but she did not release his hand as he turned. As he looked at the guests Aurora had invited. She squeezed it.

He didn't look at her. He kept his eyes on them. On the ball gowns and tiaras. The diamonds dripping from throats and fingers. On the eyes staring at him, wide with anticipation.

But he felt *her*. More than her hand holding his. *Inside* him. He squeezed her hand back and knew she felt him too. That she recognised him. And all that he was about to say wouldn't shock or appal her. He knew she had already accepted him. As he was.

And he couldn't let himself examine it any more deeply. How this realization made the ache inside him pulse with something foreign. Something he did not want to acknowledge.

He took what she offered.

Her acceptance.

That was all he wanted, not these impostors in his house.

He did not need *them* to accept him. He needed them only to know of him. Know he existed, *would exist*, with or without them. And so had Amelia.

'I am Sebastian Shard,' he said, and waited a breath too long for them to feel the weight of his name. The power of it.

His name mattered now.

He'd risen above them all from the dark places he'd called home. And he stood unflinchingly before them now as the man the forgotten boy had become.

'I am Sebastian Shard,' he said again, louder. Clearer. He would make them look now at the dirty secret they'd once preferred to ignore. 'And my mother was a prostitute. A *madam*. A pleasure provider to all those who entered her home and her body.'

The crowd gasped, and he let their shock feed him.

'I was, am, the children in your neighbourhood, and in your gated communities,' he told them, opening their ignorant eyes. 'I was nothing more than a boy, living inside a house of depravity hidden beneath your respectable veneer,' he told them. For the first time, he did not feel shamed by his past. He felt…strong.

'There are many children like the boy I was. Living

in dark spaces. Seeing unspeakable things. Ugly things. And we cannot forget them. I will not forget them.'

He inhaled deeply through flaring nostrils.

It was enough. He had said enough, told them enough.

He waved his free hand to the team of staff waiting beside the stage. He beckoned them to him with a flick of his wrist. They came. Gathered around the white cloth ten feet high behind him, concealing what he would now reveal.

He nodded, and dozens of hands pulled the cloth free until it revealed the twisted metal in all its glory. It was too tall to house in his studio, so he'd built it in the forest surrounding his home.

'It's me...' Aurora said, and he felt, heard the awe in her voice. And when he looked at her, everything, everyone else vanished.

'It is you,' he confirmed. His hands had wanted to build nothing else since the morning he'd seen her beneath his studio window. With a thousand wishes at her feet.

'Oh, Sebastian...' Her mouth parted, her eyes darting to his, then back to his creation. Metal bent to his will. He had moulded a moment. A private moment only he had seen.

'I built a thousand wishes at your feet,' he said to her. Only to her. 'Because I know, I understand, if Amelia had one wish, she would have wished for you, Aurora. Your spirit, your determination to live, to be who you are unashamed to be... Amelia would have wished for you to make me understand what was necessary. I understand now,' he said deeply. 'With your face, this sculpture, you will be the face of our new foundation to support children like her.' His throat clogged. 'Children like the boy I was.'

He turned back to the crowd, his heart raging. He raised his free hand to the walls that had been expertly lighted to showcase his art in all its forms.

'The art on the surrounding walls is yours to purchase,' he said, because he would take their money. He would take it all. 'But this—' he waved behind him '—is the symbol of our new charity. And it is called Amelia's Wish.'

He couldn't help it. His voice dried up in his throat. Something pushed it down...something he could not describe. It was light and heavy at the same time.

'Enjoy your meals,' he croaked. And pulled Aurora back the way they'd come. Down between the tables. And their eyes followed them.

Sebastian's feet faltered. Only slightly, only a tiny misstep, but Aurora's hold on him firmed as they...

Clapped.

Applauded his crude and ugly speech.

Applauded what he was and what he would now do.

For Amelia.

Hand in hand, Aurora and Sebastian made their exit out of the great hall.

He did not need their validation.

'Close the doors,' he said roughly. Shutting out their eyes, eyes he did not want on him.

He wanted her eyes.

He wanted her.

Only her.

'Aurora,' he said as the oak-and-iron doors closed behind them, the staff disappearing behind black drapes and through a side door.

'Why are we not in there?' she husked. 'You were amazing. Amelia...'

'I do not need to be in there now. I said all that had to be said.'

She swallowed thickly. 'She would be so proud of you. *I* am proud of you.' She smiled, but it quivered. Wavered.

He lifted his thumb to her lip, smoothed it across the plump softness. 'Thank you,' he said, because he knew this time, those two simple and unprofound words were enough. For her.

She kissed the tip of his thumb. Met his gaze and held it prisoner. And he was willing, he realised. A willing prisoner to her guard. He would be her captive. He would be with her. Always. Protect her with his name. His strength. The power she had unleashed within him to stand in front of them unashamed.

He dropped his thumb from her lip.

'Come to bed with me, Aurora.'

'Why?' she asked, and still her lip quivered.

'I want to take you to bed,' he said. 'I need to be with you. Naked. I want to hold you. Only you,' he said roughly. His truth. His needs. His wants.

'I was wrong,' he admitted. 'We have something special, Aurora. This, we, can work,' he said, and the word *we* did not feel stolen. It was theirs to have. 'We can be intimate. We can be friends. We can be lovers. Husband and wife. We can be a team and raise a family. The family we both want and never had before.'

They could do this.

This could work.

He knew it.

'I was wrong too,' she admitted.

He scowled. 'About what?'

'Us.'

'What about us?'

The delicate tendons in her throat tightened. 'We deserve everything.'

'I am offering you everything you asked for,' he said. 'You will never be alone or lonely. We'll be friends. We'll be intimate. We will be a family.'

'I want more.'

'There is no more.'

'There is,' she said, and her shoulders rose. Her spine straightened. 'There is love.'

'Aurora—'

She shook her head. 'I love you, Sebastian.'

Her eyes misted.

'And I need you to love me back.'

CHAPTER TWELVE

THE GROUND OPENED beneath Sebastian's feet. One step in the wrong direction, one step closer to her, and he knew he'd fall. Straight back into hell.

He released her hand.

It hurt, everywhere, to know he'd never take her hand again. Never hold it. Never feel the softness of her flawless skin press into his much rougher callused palms.

Because he had to let go.

He had to let *her* go.

'Don't.' Her grip tightened on his splayed fingers.

He would not close them.

'Don't shut me out,' she said. 'Don't… *Please*. Sebastian…'

Another broken promise.

He'd sworn never again would she beg. But here she begged him. With her big brown eyes. With her fingers holding on tightly to his.

His heart hurt. Its erratic thump was a raging beast inside him. Because here she was, begging for his love, and he couldn't give it to her. He would not. The type of love she spoke of had lived within him once, lived in his core. Love had been his purpose. And he'd needed it so much that it had destroyed him.

He wasn't so naive. He felt it again. Now. Love.

But saying it aloud, acknowledging, was different.

And he loved her too much. Too hard.

It was the same and yet different. It was a rush of warmth, of want, of need. And his hands itched to wrap themselves around it, grasp it and not let go. But he knew if he did, he would squeeze too tightly. Crush it, crush her.

He would not crush her.

'Talk to me,' she demanded. 'Scream at me. Tell me this isn't what we agreed to. This isn't what either of us wanted. But it has happened. Love. This is love,' she whispered, and it fell over his skin, draped over his shoulders. It was a heavy thing. A comforting weight.

A lie.

His love was dangerous, and to accept hers... To give her his in return, his love...

It would be a curse.

'Please, don't close me out.'

He never should have let her in.

'This was a mistake, Aurora.' Bile rose in his throat. 'I never should have listened to you scream. I never should have come out of the shadows. I never should have shown—'

'Shown me who you are?' she interrupted. 'You never should have shown me the man beneath that mask? You never should have brought me here and shown me the man inside these castle walls is a man who deserves to be loved? You deserve to be cherished, Sebastian. You deserve to be loved, and I love—'

'Stop,' he said, but the demand sounded hollow, flimsy.

'I will not stop,' she said, her other hand locking around his wrist. 'We both deserved to be loved. We were made for each other. You were made for me to love you.'

His chest caved in on itself.

If she was meant for him, if he was meant for her, then why did it hurt so much?

Because love was pain.

His love was agony.

And he would not give it to her. All this love inside him. He would not drown her in his feelings, his attachment.

He would not kill her, too.

'Aurora, release me.'

'No.'

He had to make her, didn't he? He had to make her hate him. Run from him and never look back. It was the only way to keep her safe, because now she had named it, the love they both felt, he could not protect her. Life, love, could be ripped away in an instant. It would devastate her as it had him.

It would kill him to lose her love. To lose her to the same hands of fate that had taken Amelia. But better to lose her now than fall deeper.

He moved. Stepped forward into her air. Her scent. So warm, so pure. So *innocent*. And those deep brown eyes looked up at him.

He had brought her here and locked her inside. Shut her away from the world and made her his prisoner because he thought it was the only way to keep her safe.

But he had not been keeping her safe. He had not been protecting her.

He had been protecting himself.

The world sat in the room behind them, in a great hall, and he had dragged her outside. Closed the doors on the people inside.

If he kept her here, she would always be lonely, because he did not belong with people. He did not belong in great halls.

But she did.

He had to make himself do it. *For her.* He lifted his hand and cradled her cheek. Stroked the pad of his thumb across her sculpted cheekbone.

'Sebastian…'

He leaned in until her dark lashes fluttered closed and her lips parted.

It would be so easy to close his eyes, too. To lean in those few last millimetres and claim her kiss. Claim her. Keep her here with him. But he couldn't. He knew this now.

She deserved everything.

Everything he couldn't give her.

What kind of life would she have with him? If he put his ring on her finger, what kind of life would his child have?

They deserved to live their life fully. Free. And he'd only shackle them. Keep them on the fringes, on the outside of life. Where he belonged.

But they didn't.

She didn't.

He would set her free.

'I will never love you,' he breathed, the words between her parted lips.

Her eyes flew open.

'Sebastian—'

He tightened his fingers, held her face, made her look at him.

'You think this is love?' He laced his voice with mockery, but he was only mocking himself. Because he loved her. Needed her like air.

'It was never love. It could never be love. Not between us. I brought you here to imprison you because of my baby. Never for you. Only the child. You mean nothing to me.'

'*Liar*!' she spat into his mouth.

He was a liar. It was never all about the baby. It had always been about her. But he would tell a thousand lies to save her from a life with him. He now knew it wouldn't be a life at all.

Not the life she deserved.

'I do not love you,' he said again, each word raw in his throat, his body, his mind, rejecting them as false.

It would be the only truth she knew. The only truth he would give her.

'All you are to me,' he said, and his heart raged in protest, 'is an incubator for my heir.'

She gasped, and he felt the agony in it. But it was nothing compared to the agony she'd experience if he told her his truth. That his love would suffocate her.

She loosened her hold. Released his hand. And he felt the loss of her grip deep in his bones, as if her small, delicate fingers were the only thing holding him on his feet. But he did the same. He dropped his hand from her face. He stepped back. Away from her.

He would not take her with him.

'It was all a game to you?' she said, her eyes weeping angry tears. She swiped them away with a stiff wrist. 'You played me to get the baby?'

'Yes,' he said, his body urging him to drop to his knees and beg her forgiveness. To tell her he wasn't worthy. He was sorry.

But he couldn't.

'Was it *all* a lie?' she asked.

And the answer in his mouth was instant.
That she was the only real truth he'd ever known.
She was all he wanted.
But instead of telling her that, he took another step away from her, and he knew what waited behind him as he readied himself to tell another lie.
The only lie that would protect her from *him*.
'Yes,' he said.
The hole opened wider behind him.
'It was all a lie.' he confessed the lie she needed to hear, and Sebastian took the final step.
He plunged.
Straight into hell.
And he took his love with him.

Aurora trembled. A shudder spread from deep in her abdomen until her whole body throbbed with it. With rage and confusion.

She swiped at her traitorous eyes. But she knew they revealed the truth. That beneath it all, beneath the anger heating her cheeks, it was sadness that overwhelmed her A bone-deep sadness.

It had felt so natural to tell him, to confess her love. It was the next logical step. The natural progression in their relationship. And yet…

She looked at him. Standing so close and yet feeling so far away from her.

She swallowed. Tried to stem the tremble.

He stood before her, as himself, but he was not himself.

He was cold, detached.

He was not the Sebastian she was in love with.

'It doesn't make sense,' she said out loud to herself, but he answered.

'What have I not made clear, Aurora?' he asked. 'What do you not understand?' His jaw pulsed. 'I made a mistake. We were doomed from the start. I...we...are too different. It was an error on my part. A fatal mistake to let my guard down in New York. To let you...*this* happen.' His neck corded. He shook his head. 'I was wrong. We cannot work. And I cannot pretend any longer. I can no longer perform this...*show*.'

She searched his eyes. Vacant but for the colour of his green-and-amber irises.

And suddenly it clicked.

'You were the boy in the painting, weren't you?' she asked. 'In New York. *Divinity*.'

He frowned deeply. 'What has that got to do with anything?'

'I see you.'

'I am standing right here.'

'No,' she corrected him. 'You're not. This—' she waved at the entirety of him '—is not you.'

'There is no one here but you and I.'

'It was only you and I in New York. In your studio. In my bed,' she told him. 'In the forest, by the river...' She waved at the closed doors. 'On that stage...*that* was you.' She pointed at him with trembling hands. 'This person standing in front of me is nothing more than a shell of the man I love. It is a copy of you. Wearing a mask made to deceive. But I am not deceived.'

'You deceive yourself, Aurora,' he said. 'You do not know me. You only know what I have allowed you to know.'

'I know you. I know this. These cruel words you've said to me, are...' She waved at the walls, looking for a way to explain that she knew what he was doing and she wouldn't accept it. 'Your words are nothing but a defence. Arrows you're choosing to fire at me,' she summarised for him and for herself. 'But you have missed. They have only nicked the surface. They have only inflicted flesh wounds. I am not scared. I will not run away.'

'Then you are more naive than I thought.'

'I am not naive,' she said. 'I see you.'

She would not accept this fake Sebastian when the real one, the real Sebastian, was just beneath this cruel exterior of detachment.

He was not detached. And he loved, she knew, deeply. Intensely. Desperately.

She knew he loved her. Knew it as true as she knew his baby grew inside her.

'The painting in New York... A boy in rags, his skin covered in grime... But his eyes shone. So bright. *Vivid.* They hid nothing. They let all who looked at him understand what he wanted. What he needed. If only they could look beneath their initial reaction to his condition. If they could look past the bruises beneath his tired eyes. Beneath the filth. It was there for anyone to see. For anyone to give to him. They didn't see it. But I did. I recognised it.'

'There was nothing to see in that painting. There was nothing to decode,' he said roughly. 'Nothing other than what it offered. *A painting!*'

'You're scared, aren't you?' she asked, a path clearing between all those conflicting emotions inside her that had been fogging her thoughts. 'You know I know, don't you?'

'You know nothing.'

'I do. I understand everything now. You need it still, the same thing that poor boy did, but you're scared to admit it. That the boy you were still lives inside you. And he still aches for it. Yearns for it more than anything else. He is searching for it. Begging for it. Something divine... I saw it in his eyes. And I see it in yours.'

'What are you talking about, Aurora?' he hissed. 'You are talking in riddles I do not want to understand. I do not need you to understand what the painting meant to me. *It means nothing!*'

'It's standing right in front of you,' she said, ignoring him. She knew it. Understood him more in this moment than she ever had. His search had been the same as hers. The want beneath the facade of her smiles. Her silenced voice. They both wanted it. And they could have it. They could have it all.

'I'm standing right in front of you. All you have to do is reach out and claim it. And it is yours. I am yours.'

'I have had you already, and taken all you had to give me.'

'Not this.'

'Not what?' he growled.

'Acceptance,' she husked.

'I do not need your acceptance.'

'You have it.'

'I do not want it.'

'Reach out, Sebastian. I am giving it to you. Acceptance. Love. Unconditional love.'

'Love is never enough.'

'It will be enough for us. We will have love. We will have everything we have never had before.'

'I do not...' He swallowed, and she watched the heavy drag of his Adam's apple in his throat. 'I do not love you. I do not want your love. What do I have to do to make you understand?'

'I won't let you do this, Sebastian.' She trembled. 'I

won't let you stand there and pretend you don't care. I won't let you pretend—'

'It was all a pretence,' he said. 'I do not care. I do not love you.'

'You do,' she countered breathlessly. 'You care. You love. You love me.'

'No.' He swept past her. 'It is done,' he concluded. 'We are over. It's finished.'

And her hands, her body, her heart yearned to reach out, grab him, hold him to her, until he understood she was right here with him.

She knew him.

She loved him.

But he was already walking away. Down the corridor. He was leaving her behind.

'*Sebastian*!' she called, but he didn't turn, didn't stop.

And she couldn't help it. She kicked off her pumps and gave chase.

She watched him walk through the pillared entrance to the castle and down the stone steps. And still she chased after him.

He kept going. Across the field of green. Through the artillery walls.

The pilot greeted him. Sebastian's mouth moved. She couldn't hear him. But she felt the words leave his mouth. A harsh husk of demands.

He swung open the helicopter door.

The same helicopter she'd arrived in with him.

And then he turned. Waited for her. His body was stone. His eyes dark. His jaw set.

She slowed. Breathless and panting, she tried to ground herself, to feel the short grass beneath her bare feet. But she felt nothing but a hole in her chest. And it was spreading. Hollowing her from the inside out.

She arrived in front of him, her breathing ragged and fast.

'The pilot will take you back to Arundel Manor.'

'Sebastian, please.'

'Get inside, Aurora.'

'I won't.'

'There is nothing here for you anymore,' he said. 'It was a mistake to bring you here. And now you will go back. Back to where you belong.' He didn't touch her, didn't kiss her. He simply walked away. Turned his back on her. On everything they could have.

'I belong with you,' she said to his back. 'And you belong with me.'

He halted. 'All that belongs to you,' he said, 'will be returned to you. But I will not be among your possessions. I am not something to have. I am not yours to belong to. I belong to nothing and no one.'

'And the baby?'

'Will be safer with you,' he rasped, and she heard it. The break in his voice. 'It will be happier with you.'

'There is no danger here. You are not a danger to the baby,' she said. Something broke inside her. Snapped. He was still punishing himself for a mistake he'd made when he'd been nothing but a child. 'You can't keep punishing yourself.'

He stiffened. 'My punishment is not for you to decide,' he said, and he kept walking.

'I'm not afraid of you.'

'You should be.'

'I'm not afraid to get in this helicopter,' she shouted. 'I'm not afraid to walk away.'

'Then get in,' he called back.

'You'll miss me,' she told his retreating back.

He didn't falter. 'I won't,' he said, his voice quieter now, drifting to her ears only by the grace of the wind.

'You'll come for me,' she said, but he was too far away to hear. Her voice was too weak. Unsure…

She couldn't reach him anymore.

He didn't want to be reached.

He didn't want to hear.

He didn't want to be loved.

The pilot guided her inside the helicopter, and she let him, let him buckle her in and close the door.

The helicopter's blades came to life. And up and up they went. Above the tree line. Above the castle.

She saw him. Walking up the stone steps.

She waited for him to look up. To see her.

But he didn't.

He closed the doors. Shut himself inside without her.

Her chest seized. Her lungs locked.

He'd rather be inside, locked in *with them*, than with her.

The helicopter turned. Flew away from the castle. Away from him.

A tear slipped free. She didn't brush it away. She let it slide down her cheek. Let it drip to her dress. And she acknowledged her sadness. Acknowledged his last arrow had sliced through her ribs and entered her heart.

And it was bleeding.

Her heart was shredded.

Broken.

Their time was up.

And whatever they'd had together was over.

CHAPTER THIRTEEN

Two Weeks Later...

AURORA FINGERED THE delicate yellow crib bedding tied around the antique oak bars. She pinched the soft casing that would cushion the baby from the hardwood. The tiny ducks, dancing with their open beaks sewn by hand into the bedding, taunted her with their happiness.

She turned away from it. But it was useless. In every corner of her peach bedroom, he was there. Inside the little vases. In the boxes she hadn't let them put into storage, full of the birds of prey dining set.

He'd been true to his word.

The trucks had arrived the next day.

He'd returned...*everything*. The smallest vase. The largest dining set. Her silk pumps she'd kicked off outside the great dining hall.

He'd sent it all back.

The last box had arrived today.

She looked down at her hand, at the twisted strings of silver forming the band around her middle finger.

The note had said it had been made for her, that it belonged to her, and he didn't want it.

Her heart ached. *Still.*

He didn't want her.

She splayed her fingers, flexed them. The weight felt foreign. Wrong. And she supposed it was. It was on the wrong hand. It didn't belong on that finger. It was too tight. But she couldn't bear to wear it on the right finger. The silver clawed feet holding the blue stone in the centre pinched, indented her flesh like a branding iron.

His brand.

She knew that ran deeper than the mark that would disappear when she took the ring off.

He'd changed her. Marked her as his from the first night they'd met.

And still she was his. She ached for him. In every way...

Her stomach twinged. She stroked it. But still it ached. Tightened.

'Not yet, little one,' she whispered. 'A few more days, please.'

The baby was ready, she knew. But still she held on. Still she gave him time he hadn't requested. Time she didn't have to give him.

But he wasn't coming.

Not today. Not tomorrow. Not ever.

'Ouch!' She doubled over, her hands clutched to her stomach. The Braxton Hicks contraction was tighter than usual. So tight it stole her breath.

It was only a practice contraction. It would pass. It *had* to pass. She wasn't ready. Not without him.

He *would* come. He had to.

They were not over.

They were having a baby.

They were in love.

He doesn't love you.

Pain tore through her pelvis. *'Ahh!'*

She gritted her teeth and breathed through it.

He loved her.

He loved the baby inside her.

So why isn't he here?

The pain eased. But a pressure built in her back. A weighted thing on her spine.

She sat down on the edge of the bed.

Every day, the conversation was the same. A battle of her heart and her mind. He didn't want her. He'd sent her away... And what had she done? She'd let him push her into a helicopter. She'd let him end them. Without a fight.

She closed her eyes.

She wanted *him* to fight. *For them.*

She wanted him to walk into her room, as he had all those weeks ago, and take her.

She opened her eyes, looked above the crib where she'd made them hang the painting of Sebastian. His eyes watching. When the baby was born, when their baby slept in a crib beneath it, it would remind her what was important.

Love.

Unconditional love.

A sharp pain shot up her spine.

'*Oh, oh*!' she panted. Hard and deep. The pressure was so intense in her back, her temples throbbed. Her gaze misted.

The painting wobbled.

Who had ever fought for him? For the boy longing for acceptance, for love. For support.

She wished she had a time machine. She wished she could break down the doors of the basement and save him before Amelia's birth, before he'd known such pain. And regret. And guilt.

Who had ever fought for the man?

No one.

He was still all alone in his castle, in the highest room, in the highest tower...

There they were again. Those tears she didn't want, hot on her flushed cheeks. And she knew she had a choice.

She could wail. She could scream. Or she could accept it. The end of them. She could move on. Raise her child on her own. She would live, she'd exist with or without Sebastian.

She couldn't make him make the right choice.

She couldn't make him love her.

She couldn't make him accept her love.

But *she* could fight. She could fight the demons he still battled for him. She could protect him with her love. She could love him. Harder than he had ever known love.

A moan slipped from her lips. And it wasn't the physical pain crushing her hips in a vice grip. It was the pain of realizing her stupidity.

She was stupid. Blind.

She didn't need to be rescued.

He did.

All her life, she'd accepted things. The way she was supposed to behave. The choices she'd had to agree to. And all her life, she'd been on the outside of her own life. Waiting. Waiting for her parents' love and acceptance. She'd smiled through her pain, nodded when she'd disagreed with the ugly choices she'd been made to accept because she'd been too afraid to fight for what she believed in.

But she believed in her and Sebastian.

In their love.

What was she waiting for? For permission to love him? He'd never give it to her without a fight.

She'd been fighting for them, she realised, since the night they met. Fighting for all they could be together. In the gardens. In the castle. And all the little fights that had led to this. The final battle she would need to win.

What weapons did she have?

Only herself.

Only her love.

He was sleeping beauty.

And she would wake him.

She reached for her phone next to the bed.

She couldn't even call him—she didn't have his number.

But Esther would. Esther would help her.

She rang the number she'd rung so many times during the week of the gala.

And she waited.

'Aurora.'

'Can you get me a helicopter?'

'Why are you so breathless?' Esther asked.

Was she?

'I need to go to him…' Her head swam. 'Now.'

The line went silent, and Aurora's heart throbbed.

She could get herself a helicopter. She'd never used one for herself. She didn't have one in the garden. Esther could arrange it faster.

'Please,' Aurora sobbed. 'He's all alone. He shouldn't be alone.'

'No, he shouldn't,' Esther agreed. 'I can get one for you. Are you at home? At the manor?'

The tears were back, but her smile was new. And it

felt good to smile. To know that soon she would be with him. Where she belonged.

'Yes.'

'Stay on the line,' Esther said. 'I'll tell you how long it will be.'

'Make it soon,' she said.

'As soon as I can,' she promised, and Aurora almost jumped for joy, but she was too tired, too swollen and pregnant to do so.

She needed to get ready. She put her hand on the side of the bed and pushed—

Aurora's blood ran cold.

'Esther...'

'I'm still here.'

She sat back down on the bed. Reached for the part of her light blue dress now stained a deep red.

She lifted her fingers to her face. 'I'm bleeding.'

'*Bleeding*?' Esther demanded. 'Where from?'

She couldn't breathe. Her head was fuzzy. A deep fog was falling over her, making everything heavy. Everything weak.

'The baby,' she breathed, and it trembled from her lips. 'The baby, Esther...'

And then she could speak no more words.

The phone fell.

And so too did Aurora.

Sebastian was cold.

He knew he'd never be warm again.

He deserved to be cold. To sit here in the abandoned great dining hall, all alone, and freeze.

He probably would.

He turned up the collar on his brown winter fur. The

same one he'd laid Aurora's head upon as he'd kissed her. Found pleasure in her, made love to her.

He closed his eyes. Shut out the empty tables. The empty room.

He'd sent them all away. And they had gone. Esther had taken all his art. All of it had sold the minute he'd left the stage with Aurora.

She'd taken his sculpture, too. It was placed inside the entrance to the building Esther had acquired for him for the headquarters of the charity he was now the face of. And *her* face would be the symbol for it. A symbol of hope for all those who needed it.

Amelia's Wish would be a success. A charity he should have set up the moment he'd been able to. He realised that now.

He realized it because of *her*.

Aurora.

It didn't matter how tightly he squeezed his eyes shut. She was always there. Burnt onto his retinas since the first time he'd turned his head and laid his gaze upon her.

She did not bring him hope.

She was his torment. His endless torture. His punishment.

And this was hell.

His heart hurt. It had not stopped hurting since she'd left. Since he'd forced her to go.

And he endured the hurt, because it was his to endure.

He'd spared her from sharing his fate. He'd saved her, and their child, from living this life with him. They did not deserve to share in his life sentence in this desolate place where nothing lived but pain.

It was the one good thing he'd ever done.

He had not done what he'd wanted to. He had had not

crushed her with his love. Suffocated her with his greed to have her, hold her, always.

He had set her free.

And he could barely breathe. The air was too thin without her. His lungs strained for just a single breath of her. His skin ached for her softness. *Her closeness*.

He'd never be close to her again. He'd never touch her. He'd never again breathe in her scent.

The reckoning was over.

Her job was done.

She had made him acknowledge all of his misdeeds. Brought them back into his present, and he had faced them. And now he would pay for what he'd done.

She had woken him from a deep, dark slumber of self-pity.

But now he was always awake. Would always be aware of what he'd done.

What he had almost done to her too. Locked her away, like he'd locked himself away. Kept her in the dark with him. But she deserved the light. So much of it.

He deserved the dark. He did not know how to live amongst other people with her.

His back pocket pulsed, vibrated furiously.

Again and again.

Sebastian pulled his phone free of his pocket.

'Esther,' he said, holding the phone to his ear.

'Don't panic,' she said.

'Why would I panic?' he replied. 'I do not panic.'

'She's okay,' she said, ignoring him. 'Or she will be. She was bleeding heavily. She's at the hospital. I'm on my way now.'

His blood roared. 'Where is she?'

'Cirencester. Private Hospital.'

He stood, his body moving on instinct to get to her. To be with her.

'I am on my way,' he said, and his voice was tight, weak.

He had been too weak, hadn't he?

Too afraid to fight for her.

For *her* love.

And now…

His throat squeezed. Threatening to crush his airways.

He burst through the entrance doors. They banged open. And he left them that way. Wide open as ran down the stone steps.

'The helicopter should be landing now,' Esther said. 'Can you see it?'

He could.

He could see it all.

His fear. Her strength. Their love. Rare and divine. She was everything he'd ever wanted.

And now he could lose it all.

He could lose her.

CHAPTER FOURTEEN

SEBASTIAN BURST THROUGH the hospital doors in his long brown fur coat and big black boots.

He steeled his spine, broadened his shoulders, and readied himself for the smoke. For the flames. For the chaos. His heart gushed. He could not ready himself for that. For loss.

He could not lose Aurora.

His breath snagged in his lungs. All was still. All was quiet. People sat on cream sofas, and they smiled and talked in gentle whispers. Others walked through the flowerpotted corridor as if nothing was happening. As if his Aurora was not bleeding. As if his love, his only love, was not dying. Without him.

'Aurora!' It was bellow, a scream, louder, rawer than the one he had screamed to the skies, to the gods, the morning Amelia had died.

Aurora would not die.

He would not allow it.

He would forsake the gods.

He would make them bring her back.

All eyes turned to him. Mouths dropped. A man in black walked towards him. His shoulders squared.

A guard wouldn't stop him.

'Where is she?' Sebastian demanded.

'He's with me.' Esther suddenly appeared behind the man. Her perfect black bob cut slashed across her determined brown-skinned jaw. She walked toward him. Looked up into his face, which was still staring down the man who barred his way to Aurora. But she was here. In one of these rooms. And he would find her.

She gripped his elbow. 'He's with me,' she said again, and he could not examine it. He could not think clearly. He could only think of Aurora. She needed him. And he was too late. But it meant something. Esther holding his elbow, claiming him as hers. Protecting him from confrontation.

'He's the father,' she continued. 'Aurora Arundel,' she explained. 'She's in recovery.'

The rage that filled his vision, aimed at this stranger, this man who meant him no harm, whose job it was to protect those in the hospital, dissipated.

Sebastian's shoulders sagged. He dropped his gaze to Esther's wide brown eyes. Bruises sat beneath her usually immaculately made-up eyes. Tightness bracketed her colourless mouth.

'Recovery?' he asked, and it was a prayer on his lips. 'She's...she's alive?'

She nodded. 'She's alive.'

Alive... She wasn't dead. She was not lost to him.

'Take me to her.'

Esther shook her head. 'She needs a little time.'

There was no time. He was already late. She was hurting. He'd sent her away to protect her, but he hadn't, he couldn't...

He could not breathe.

He'd failed her.

'Take me to her,' he demanded. *'Now.'*

He needed to see her. To know she was alive. To hold her. Breathe her in and fall to his knees, and beg for her forgiveness.

He had been wrong. So very wrong to send her away.

He would follow her everywhere she went now.

He would follow her into the light and let the sun flay the skin from his flesh, if that is what it took to be with her.

Esther's fingers tightened on his elbow. 'There's someone you should meet first.'

'Who?' he growled.

A tear slipped from the corner of her eye.

'Your son.'

'My son?' he repeated, and he couldn't fight it.

Amelia, clear as the day she was born, formed in his mind. Her tiny fingers. Her innocent eyes. He'd loved her instantly. And he couldn't ignore it. The fear in his gut. What if he couldn't give his baby the same?

What if he could not love his son?

'This way,' Esther said, and she led him down the corridor.

'He's in here,' she said, stopping.

She held the door open for him. The bed was empty, but beside it sat a crib on wheels. A hand, so small, fingers so tiny, peeped out at him over the rim.

He rushed to the crib and peered inside…

His heart burst.

He was perfection. He was… He had Aurora's black hair, thick and too long for a newborn. He had a little button nose, plum lips. But his eyes, they were just like Sebastian's.

And he vowed right there and then, his little eyes would never see the horrors his father had.

He dipped his hands inside, and he picked up his son. Claimed him. He brought him to his chest. Cradled him, kept him warm beneath the brown furs he wore.

It was instant.

The love.

The unconditional love.

Sebastian turned to Esther. Tears filled his eyes. 'I have a son.'

'You do.' She smiled, flaunted all of her perfectly square teeth as her eyes cried. 'Congratulations, Sebastian. You're a father.'

Sebastian closed his eyes.

And he wept.

All the tears he hadn't before been able to. For the boy he had been. For Amelia. For his son. For Aurora. And he cried, too, for love.

The love in his heart. The love all around him, in the touch of his son, in Esther's eyes. And they offered him nothing but warmth. Acceptance.

He knew he would never be cold again.

He was loved.

He loved them all, he realised.

Had she lifted the curse?

Had Aurora set him free?

Aurora opened her eyes. Soft amber lights lit the space. A room as big as any hotel room. A blue vertical tunnel sat in the room's corner.

She watched the bubbles rise in the softly swirling water. Let her eyes adjust to being here. To still being alive. To surviving. She breathed in deeply. Felt her lungs rise and fall. Her fingers gripped something too soft, too familiar. A brown blanket of the softest fur covered her body.

She was alive. But…

Her chest thumping, she turned her head to the side of the bed, to where the crib should be. Where her baby should be.

And her heart, it swelled.

There was her son. On his father's chest. His black-capped head cradled in a big, wide hand. A hand holding him so carefully, so gently, against his heart.

The heart he wouldn't let her have.

Sebastian's head lay back against the green leather of the high-backed armchair, his hair cushioning his cheek, and it fell to his shoulder.

They both slept so peacefully together.

His eyes opened. His green-rimmed irises made the inner amber of his eyes glow.

'Forgive me,' he growled.

'You're here,' she said, her heart aching for him. He had punished himself enough. 'You found us. There is nothing to forgive.'

His gaze sharpened. 'There is *everything* to forgive.'

He went to stand.

'Don't,' she said. 'You'll wake him,'

'I won't.' He stood, moved to her bedside, and he did not wake the baby as he placed him in Aurora's arms. 'He should be in your arms. Where he is safe.'

And her heart, it could not take it. How could she make him understand he wasn't a danger? To either of them?

'He's so small,' she said. 'So precious.' And she held him close. Her son. The baby she had carried inside her for all those months. The baby that had brought Sebastian back to her. The baby that would make them a family. She pressed her lips to his head. Kissed him with all the love she had saved for him. Only the baby. But she had more love to give. More love to share with Sebastian. Her true love.

She raised her eyes to his. 'But he *is* safe with you,' she told him. 'We both are.'

He nodded. 'I know.'

'You do?'

'I know many things,' he replied. 'Because of you.'

'What else do you know?' she asked.

He sat down on the edge of the bed. And Aurora wanted to yell at him, to scream at him to choose everything. Now. With her. But she didn't scream. She didn't yell. She waited for him. Gave him time to tell her.

Because she would wait for him to be ready.

She'd wait for him for what felt like forever.

'I lied,' he said, and held her gaze. 'Amelia didn't wish for you. *I did.* Twenty-five years ago, I asked the gods, *I begged them*, for you, and they delivered my wish. They delivered you for me.'

Her heart broke for him. For all those years he'd spent alone. Waiting for…her.

'I'm sorry I was late.'

'I wasn't ready.' He shook his head. 'But I am ready now. I'm ready to change. For you. For our son.'

'I don't want you to change.'

'But I will,' he said. 'I will open the doors. I will let love in, and I will not suffocate it. I will not kill it. I will cherish it.'

'I need more than softness, Sebastian,' she said. 'I need your love.' She swallowed. 'I want your heart.'

'And it is yours. It was always yours,' he confessed.

'I knew it from the moment I saw you. I know that now. I understand I was too afraid to call it love. To name it. Claim it. I was scared that if I loved you as I loved Amelia, I would have to forever lock you inside a room to protect you. I would suffocate you with my love. So I sent you away. Both of you.' His nostrils flared. 'But I love you, Aurora. More than the air in my lungs. I am sorry I sent you away. I am sorry I pushed you away so many times when you only wanted to hold me. Let me hold you now, Aurora,' he begged. 'Let me love you.'

Her heart bloomed as she held the baby against her breast with one hand, and she held the other open for him to join them.

'Come to me,' she said, and his eyes glistened as he did just that. Leaned into her. Moved his mouth until it sat a hair's breadth away from hers. He breathed, 'I will always love you, Aurora. You were made for me to love. And I will love you with everything I am for the rest of my life.'

Gently he feathered his lips against hers. 'If you still want me to?' he asked roughly. His voice raw. 'If you can still love me?'

'I'll always love you, Sebastian.' She reached up to his face, and the air stilled. As did her heart. 'You were made for me to love. I was made for you to love.'

'Aurora…'

She didn't know who moved first. And she held his face, cradled it, as he gave to her all that was inside him.

His love.

His heart.

'I love you,' he breathed into her mouth.

And she understood time had reset.

Theirs was just beginning.

EPILOGUE

Six Months Later...

BLACK PILLAR LAMPPOSTS of knotted metal with glass tops lit the space. Dew clung to the leaves. Newly emerging buds lifted upwards to meet the sun. And the fireflies danced on the walls.

He'd replicated it perfectly. And yet it was different. They would not meet in the dark. He had all the lights on. There was no key in the gold lock. The black iron gates, bracketed by headed stone pillars, were wide open.

He was not hiding in the shadows of the colonnade.

He stood on the stone path, and he waited for her.

He would see her. She would see him. And they would meet here, in the gardens, where it had all begun.

Sebastian let his gaze wander over the walled garden of wild flowers. They had been trimmed and harnessed to allow for the small gathering of white chairs tied with silver bows. For the arch of wild flowers they'd meet beneath. But it was still wild. And he recognised it now, saw it. Its beauty. Because in all things wild, there was a stillness. A harmony.

Aurora was his stillness. She was his harmony. He was

calm. He wore no other skin than his own. And he did not feel wild or tamed. He felt...*whole*. Seen.

His throat tightened.

His eyes fell on Esther and her wife. Their only guests. Together, they held his son for him. Protected him with their love for him, their love for each other, and their love for... *Sebastian*. And he accepted it. Esther's loyalty. Her love. And he gave it back tenfold. She was... *they* were...his family.

He was loved, and he loved. Deeply. He accepted that now. Accepted what he hadn't been able to accept for twenty-five years—that he was not cursed to kill with his love. He was not blinded by feelings. His feelings made him stronger. His love was the precursor to everything he'd never had, but all he would have now with Aurora. A family.

All the air left his lungs in a hiss.

Through the iron gates, she came to him.

And Sebastian watched her. Pearls dotted her black hair, which was tied in a loose knot at the side of her head. A few silken locks fell forward to kiss her cheeks. Strands of smaller pearls hung from her ears. The white fur cape hanging from her shoulders moved in time with her white satin shoes. Her dress, sculpted to her body, was made of the iridescent pearls of the sea.

His siren had returned, and he would go with her willingly.

Because wherever she was, he was home.

She was his home.

She was his family.

Aurora *was* love.

His love.

He was born to love her. Made only for her. All he had

been through, all he had endured, was to prepare him for how hard he could love.

And it was so very intensely. So very hard that he loved her.

She was his. She belonged to him, and he belonged to her.

And there on the broken stone path where they had met, they shared their vows and joined their hands in matrimony.

In love.
Unconditional love.
Forever.

* * * * *

Did you fall head over heels for
Kidnapped for Her Secret?
Then don't miss these other dazzlingly dramatic stories by Lela May Wight!

His Desert Bride by Demand
Bound by a Sicilian Secret
The King She Shouldn't Crave
Italian Wife Wanted

Available now!

Get up to 4 Free Books!

We'll send you 2 free books from each series you try
PLUS a free Mystery Gift.

FREE Value Over **$25**

Both the **Harlequin Presents** and **Harlequin Medical Romance** series feature exciting stories of passion and drama.

YES! Please send me 2 FREE novels from Harlequin Presents or Harlequin Medical Romance and my FREE gift (gift is worth about $10 retail). After receiving them, if I don't wish to receive any more books, I can return the shipping statement marked "cancel." If I don't cancel, I will receive 6 brand-new larger-print novels every month and be billed just $7.19 each in the U.S., or $7.99 each in Canada, or 4 brand-new Harlequin Medical Romance Larger-Print books every month and be billed just $7.19 each in the U.S. or $7.99 each in Canada, a savings of 20% off the cover price. It's quite a bargain! Shipping and handling is just 50¢ per book in the U.S. and $1.25 per book in Canada.* I understand that accepting the 2 free books and gift places me under no obligation to buy anything. I can always return a shipment and cancel at any time. The free books and gift are mine to keep no matter what I decide.

Choose one:
- ☐ **Harlequin Presents Larger-Print** (176/376 BPA G36Y)
- ☐ **Harlequin Medical Romance** (171/371 BPA G36Y)
- ☐ **Or Try Both!** (176/376 & 171/371 BPA G36Z)

Name (please print)

Address   Apt. #

City   State/Province   Zip/Postal Code

Email: Please check this box ☐ if you would like to receive newsletters and promotional emails from Harlequin Enterprises ULC and its affiliates. You can unsubscribe anytime.

Mail to the **Harlequin Reader Service:**
IN U.S.A.: P.O. Box 1341, Buffalo, NY 14240-8531
IN CANADA: P.O. Box 603, Fort Erie, Ontario L2A 5X3

Want to explore our other series or interested in ebooks? Visit www.ReaderService.com or call 1-800-873-8635.

---

*Terms and prices subject to change without notice. Prices do not include sales taxes, which will be charged (if applicable) based on your state or country of residence. Canadian residents will be charged applicable taxes. Offer not valid in Quebec. This offer is limited to one order per household. Books received may not be as shown. Not valid for current subscribers to the Harlequin Presents or Harlequin Medical Romance series. All orders subject to approval. Credit or debit balances in a customer's account(s) may be offset by any other outstanding balance owed by or to the customer. Please allow 4 to 6 weeks for delivery. Offer available while quantities last.

Your Privacy—Your information is being collected by Harlequin Enterprises ULC, operating as Harlequin Reader Service. For a complete summary of the information we collect, how we use this information and to whom it is disclosed, please visit our privacy notice located at https://corporate.harlequin.com/privacy-notice. Notice to California Residents – Under California law, you have specific rights to control and access your data. For more information on these rights and how to exercise them, visit https://corporate.harlequin.com/california-privacy. For additional information for residents of other U.S. states that provide their residents with certain rights with respect to personal data, visit https://corporate.harlequin.com/other-state-residents-privacy-rights/.

HPHM25